BRUISE

Desiree Bissonnette

authorHOUSE®

AuthorHouse™ LLC
1663 Liberty Drive
Bloomington, IN 47403
www.authorhouse.com
Phone: 1-800-839-8640

Published by AuthorHouse 09/11/2014

ISBN: 978-1-4969-3934-0 (sc)
ISBN: 978-1-4969-3933-3 (hc)
ISBN: 978-1-4969-3932-6 (e)

Library of Congress Control Number: 2014916170

1

I don't want to wake up today. Really, I don't want to leave my bed for anything, even though I know I have to. School won't accept my excuse for avoiding it, because the only one I have is "too sad to function" and that's not valid to anyone but me. They stopped giving a shit when I entered high school. Avoiding school because of bullying problems as a kid is one thing, but as soon as you're older you're supposed to get over it. I'm a big girl now; I have to get over it. No one will accept depression as an excuse to miss work. I'll have to face the real world soon, and the real world doesn't care if I think I'm sad. I'll have to get over it.

That's what my counsellor and parents tell me all the time anyways. That's what everyone has told me, even if it was none of their business in the first place. Every time I've gone to talk to anyone about it, it's always been the same. People keep telling me that happiness is a choice, and that if I don't choose now I'll never be happy. Then they load me up on medication to help my brain function like a normal person's, which doesn't always work. My brain is stubborn, and the voices are loud.

I'm not crazy or anything, that I'm sure of. The "voices" are me; hundreds of me's that try to pull me in all directions. Some towards getting through the day, others hell-bent on ending it forever. They tell me to get up, to get moving, to be normal, to be happy; anything and everything I feel I can't do myself I have to constantly remind myself to do.

Get up Sara. Come on, get up.

Waking up has proven itself to be both the easiest and the hardest part of my day. Easiest because I don't have to deal with anyone but myself and sometimes my cat Lou. Hardest because I have to make an effort to wake up, get up and do something, and then make an effort to do that everyday. But that's why I have the voices; they help me get okay. I help me get okay.

Wake up Sara. Get up Sara. Go outside Sara. Don't forget to smile. You're okay.

The clock on my nightstand starts blaring like an air raid siren. I slam my fist down hard on it, cracking the plastic and possibly some of the bones in my pinkie. I start clenching and unclenching my hand.

Now I'm awake. I'm alive. Both kind of suck.

But you're a big girl now; you have to get over it.

I reach for the nightstand again and grab my phone. I click the top button to turn on the screen, but it blinds me and I drop it on my face. I can already tell that today is going to be just peachy. The universe must want me to stay in bed today too. For the first time in a long time we agree on something.

I pick up the phone again and wait for my eyes to adjust to the brightness of the screen. I have 4 messages and, not to my surprise at all, they're all from Colten.

Colten Shepard, 12:30 am
Goodnight babe <3
Colten Shepard, 4:30 am
Hey, you awake?
Colten Shepard, 4:40 am
Guess not . . .
Colten Shepard, 6:02 am
Good morning beautiful:)

It sounds rude, but the first thing I do is roll my eyes. We aren't together, or in love. I'm not anyways. To me he's just a friend with too many expectations and stupid romantic ideas about things that have no business being romanticized. I don't want to reply to him; the last thing he needs is me talking to him after he calls me some girly pet name, but my phone's iMessage has already shot that horse in the face. I have to reply, or risk some awkward confrontation later.

Me, 6:35 am
Hey.
Colten Shepard, 6:35 am
How are you this morning? Did you have a good sleep?
Me, 6:38 am
I'm okay. It was alright
Colten Shepard, 6:39 am

Want a ride to school?
Me, 6:41 am
No I'm fine. Thanks for the offer though.
Colten Shepard, 6:42 am
O . . . Ok. C u at school.

I put my phone down and exhale deeply. He's upset. He only ever types like a 12 year old going through "the phase" when he's upset. He's immature in that way, because he knows it makes me feel bad when he acts like he's been hurt. It's happened countless times in our relationship regardless of my feelings. Every rejection I've given him for anything, especially "more than friends proposals", has ended with him acting like I've broken his spirit beyond repair. I can't stand him when he acts like this. I can't stand him half of the time, regardless.

I chuckle a little at that; the only person who takes time out of their day to try to be my friend, and I can't stand him. It's not because he's a bad person.

He can get pretty bad when he pulls the friend zone bullshit out and rubs it around in my face, but the real reason I can't handle being around him is the he wants me to be hopelessly in love with him to the point where my depression goes away. Somewhere in his mind when I began to open up to him he rationalized that his feelings for me were the cure for everything. But life isn't like that, and no feelings from him will ever remedy anything. He's blind to it though, and pursues me nonetheless with promises of happiness and other bullshit. The reality is that his "love will fix you" mindset makes me feel worse about myself and about our friendship.

But he tries to be my friend, and that's got to count for something, even if it's a small something. He's one of the few that protects me from the Queen Bee, and that's a comfort to me, even though his fondness of me only makes her hate me more. Her crush on him was part of what started her relentless hatred of me. I can remember the day she told me she liked him like it was yesterday, and I can remember the day she started to hate me because of it even clearer. I had no idea how hard the Queen Bee would sting me because I was existing too close to Colten.

I put my hands over my eyes and run them through my hair. Thinking about her stresses me out. I have to get over it though.

I look over at the clock and sigh. 7:00AM. I've procrastinated getting up as long as I should allow myself to.

Get up Sara. Time to get up.

3

I sit up in my bed and pull my comforter off as fast as I can. My room feels freezing without it, and I'm woken up almost immediately from the rush. It's still too dark in my room to see anything, but turning on the light or opening the curtains will only make my eyes sting. I wobble blindly towards my door, stepping on dirty discarded clothes and clothes that I didn't bother to put away after washing. When I reach the door I open it slowly, careful not to make much noise. I don't want my mom to know I'm awake until I've gotten out of the shower.

It's not a short walk from my room to the bathroom but my head is spinning enough to make it feel like a kilometre. The hallway is dark and the light of the bathroom creeps along the wall, waiting to blind me. I push the slightly ajar door open with my finger tips.

Yeah, blinded.

My eyes adjust to the bathroom light and soon I'm staring at a tiny girl in the mirror. She could be pretty, if she tried. Her face is round, framed by a pitch black pixie cut with bright blue highlights. They look as artificial as her weak smile. Her upper lip is thin and wispy, contrasting the plumpness of her lower lip. Her skin is dark, olive coloured and she has thick eyebrows that arch gently over her dull grey eyes. I stare at her and criticize her nose, which seems a little bulbous at the end and points upwards farther than it seems it should. There's a bump on it where a stud used to dig into her skin before it was replaced with a ring, and a huge birthmark towards the top of the bridge that makes it look like she's got some kind of blotchy skin condition; but she could be pretty if she tried to be.

Too bad I'm not going to try to be.

When I open the bathroom cabinet, I'm greeted by a mass of pill bottles that range from Tylenol to Midol and back again. My mother is adamant on always having them around just in case her head or her uterus decide to go at war with her. I like to tough my pain out. The only thing I can't tough out is my depression, and for that I have bupropion to help. I reach for the bottle at the back of the cabinet and take the tiny whit tablet into my hand.

Take it.

I swallow the tablet hard and stare at myself in the mirror.

You're going to be okay.

I strip down and jump into the shower, which in retrospect is a stupid idea because the water is always cold when you first turn it on. But it still feels nice, and as it warms up I sit down in the tub and get comfortable. The shower is my favourite place in the world. It's the only place I feel safe half the time. No one walks into the bathroom when you're in the shower, at least not in my family. If I'm in the shower, I'm free to cry and hurt myself and scream if I want, and all I need to cover my tracks is my music player and a bathrobe.

I used to hurt myself in my room when I started. I think the first time I did it I was 13, and I had just been labelled the Super Dyke at my school by Queen Bee because she stole my people notebook in class and read some of the passages I had written while people watching. I had written about a girl I had seen who I thought was hot, and she plastered it around the school for everyone to see. I wasn't mad about being called a lesbian, because I'm not but and being gay isn't an insult, I was mad that she was causing so many problems for me because of it, and I was mad that she was making me seem like a villain for being attracted to girls. After all she and I had been through, she made me feel bad about being myself for the first time, and everyone joined in on it. For almost 3 weeks everyday whispers chased my heels in the hallway, people pushed into me and knocked my books out of my arms, and I was looked at like some caged zoo animal with a disease. Everyone began feeding the void that had already started growing inside of me with their hate and I absorbed it all like a sponge. I was angry and hurt and the only person I felt I could take it out on was myself. I made the first cut into my wrist, which is the stupidest idea because I realized shortly after that I could actually die. Back then I didn't want to die. Oh how far I've come since then.

Get over it Sara. Don't think about that Sara.

My mom found me in my room screaming and crying, and they took me to the hospital. Then the psychiatrist. Then the principal. I got put under suicide watch, and after that I tried to hide them. Whenever my parents would find them they'd think I was trying to get attention, and they'd get angry at me. That's when I started hiding them better, and only doing it in the bathroom. Can't yell at me for what you can't see. No mess no hassle.

I hate how much I like the feeling, even now. Since the beginning of the year I've tried to stop, but I relapse often

Stop thinking about it now Sara.

The water is starting to get cooler but I still don't want to leave the shower. When I leave I'll have to do things. I'll have to talk to people, and I'll have to pretend to be happy again and I'm just not ready for that. I don't think I'll ever be ready to pretend again. I'm so sick of pretending. I'm not very good at it either.

Get out of the shower now Sara. Come on, time to go.

I get out of the shower and turn the water off. As soon as the sound of running water is silenced, I can hear scratching at the door and I already know it's my jackass of a cat Lou. He has a serious problem with personal space, as in he doesn't know anyone has it and will relentlessly pursue you for pets. I open the door for him, and he strolls into the bathroom, his orange furred fat stomach giggling around like jelly in an earthquake. Disgusting, but still so adorable. He rubs against my legs and wads of fur stick to them, dampening as they touch my skin. Lou purrs loudly, but I kick him away gently. He curls himself up on the toilet seat and stares at me. Lou is a pervert.

If Lou is up and about it means that my mother will be downstairs, probably making breakfast or trying to refuel herself on caffeine before she goes to Tim Horton's for more caffeine. She calls it a "Canadian morning ritual", but I call it an addiction.

Okay Sara, time to go downstairs. Go downstairs now.

2

When I go downstairs I'm hit with a wave of vanilla scented breakfast bliss. My mother, who already looks like the Native American version of Betty Crocker, is in the kitchen flipping pancakes like the world is ending. She's wearing her pink frilly apron that dad bought her for Christmas almost 6 years ago, completing her housewife look. Good job saying no to gender roles mom.

My parents are the personification of gender roles in their own way. My mom bakes, works with kids as a day care operator and cleans everything with precise obsession. It's not healthy, I think anyways. My dad on the other hand, is the bacon bringer with his high end teacher job at the catholic high school that has a total of 5 good catholic students. I've always thought they expected me to be a part of their perfect family stereotype. I'm almost sure of it. They'd be happy if their daughter wasn't a depressed loser with shitty grades and a heteronormative sexual preference, but they got me. Poor Hale family.

Just get over it Sara. Don't think about it Sara.

"Good morning sweetie," my mom says, smiling wide. I smile back, and take a seat at the table. The second my butt touches the chair, I've already got three pancakes stacked in front of me and a glass of orange juice filled to the rim.

Housewives, I think, rolling my eyes. My mom doesn't notice. She's too busy flipping pancakes for the army she's feeding in her head. There's only the three of us and Lou, so her overzealous amount of pancakes is unnecessary. Lou is going to have a heyday eating all of these, as he usually gets anything we don't eat. Lou is probably one of the luckiest cats suffering from obesity in all of Canada.

"What's with the pancakes?" I ask. While my mother is often in the kitchen cooking meals for me and my dad, vanilla pancakes are a rarity. We have them for three occasions; holidays, birthdays, and when

7

someone I know dies. Vanilla pancakes are not Thursday mornings, they are "grandma died and we don't know how to tell you" mornings. I'm all out of grandparents to eat pancakes to, and as far as I'm aware it's not a holiday. Maybe some obscure American holiday, but not one that I would celebrate.

"It's the school dance this week! I know it's seems like I'm over doing it, but I'm just too excited," she says, waving her fists in the air. She looks like a little girl who just got a pony. The dance is not a holiday.

Calm down Sara.

"Too bad I'm not going," I say, stuffing one of my pancakes in my mouth. My mom's nose scrunches up because she hates when I don't use utensils. I hate when she tries to get me to socialize, and since I know what's coming next I can afford to be gross.

"Sara Kaitlyn Hale, you can't miss out on your senior prom."

"No really, I can. And intend to."

Her mouth tightens into a straight line and she breathes loudly out of her nose. Sometimes my mom acts like she's younger than me, and she looks young enough to get away with it. I look up at her and take in her youth. She looks like me, but her green eyes are brighter and full of life. Her skin is darker than mine is, because of her Cree heritage, and dotted with age spots and crow's feet. Her face is sharp, almost mousy, and her dark curls are pulled into a messy mom bun. She looks at me and scrunches her thin eyebrows.

"Is it because of A-"

"Mom can you not talk about her, please? She's not the reason I don't want to go okay?"

"Then why don't you want to go?" she asks, and I start rolling the reasons out in my head. Queen Bee and her drones buzzing around, Colten being a friend zoned douche again, talking to people, loud music, drunken teenagers sneaking in. Drugs probably. Social interaction and having to dress up formally. Missing the next episode of Doctor Who on Netflix. There aren't enough reasons for me TO go.

Get over it Sara you have to try.

"Mom, dances are for popular kids who have dates and want to experiment with drugs and sex," I say, hoping that it will put her out of the mindset of me needing to go. The last thing they want me doing is having sex, even though that ship has sailed. I still wear the creepy purity ring they made me get as a kid. When you're younger you don't even realize that Purity Balls are fucked up, but my parents made me go to one and my dad pledged to protect the purity of my mind, body and soul. He isn't very good at it either, I mean—look at me. If my mind were pure I wouldn't be so fucked up in the head. I'd be normal, and not such a piece of shit.

Don't degrade yourself Sara. Stop that.

"Then it's a good thing you're not like those kids. We didn't raise you to be like that," say says, and wipes her hands on a hand towel before tucking it into her apron. I take another bite of a pancake because I don't want to say anything to her. If I told her what I was thinking I'm sure she'd slap me.

You didn't raise me to be depressed either but here I am, I think. My mom gives me an unimpressed look. Sometimes I think she can hear thoughts. She sighs as loud as she can, and sits across from me at the table. I try to focus on eating my breakfast, but our conversation has seriously killed my appetite.

You need to eat, Sara.

"Why is everything so hard for you Sara?"

Yeah Sara, suck it up.

I shrug. My mom sighs again.

"Didn't Colten ask you to go with him? He seems like such a sweet boy."

"Yeah he *seems* sweet mom, but he's not very good at handling rejection and I'd rather not deal with him acting like a little kid."

That sets her off on one of my least favourite speech, which I've learned to tune out when she starts. Why don't you give him a chance? So many girls would feel so lucky to be in your position. He's so nice to you. I can tell he really likes you. Don't be so difficult blah blah blah blah blah. It's like watching Charlie Brown on max volume, but only being able to watch the scenes with the adults of the show.

"Wah wah, wah wah wah wah wah?" My mom says.

"No," I say.

"Wah wah wah," my mom says, angrily. She's getting impatient with me.

"I gotta rock—go. I've got to go," I say. My mom fakes a smile, but I know she's being insincere about it.

"Have a good day honey. Just think about going to the dance? Please? I've already gone out and bought you a dress. We can do your hair and make-up all nice . . . You can be normal."

"Whatever," I say, but I'm not going to think about the dance at all. I don't want to think about the dance. It's a disaster waiting to happen.

Get over it Sara, just go. Just try.

My mom gets up to hug me but I leave before she can reach me. Outside it's nice, surprising for April, which is usually full of snow and fog and other crappy weather. I walk across the grass and on to the sidewalk, and start towards the direction of the school. It's not much of a walk from my house to the school, but there's a Tim Horton's on the way which delays my travel time by a few minutes everyday.

It's always the same thing for me; a large black coffee. Since my classes don't start until 9, I'll usually sit in the restaurant for half an hour and watch frustrated white Canadians scream at panicked Filipino Canadians that their coffee isn't right. Canadians take their coffee as seriously as their hockey, and it's scary to mess with that. The few times I've seen Canadians be incredibly rude and racist is because of coffee, and it's always been incredibly embarrassing to me. It's bean water. Get over it Canada.

Get over it Sara. It's none of your business.

When I get to Tim's the place is busy, as it usually is in the morning. Some of the people in line are still in their pyjamas rubbing sleep out of their eyes and yawning. The woman in front of me is holding two toddlers on leashes, reeling them in as they try to scurry away from her like prisoners running from cops. She barks angry words at them, and I can't help but think she should be the one on the leash.

By the time I get to the front of the line, the cashier already has my order waiting for me. He's an attractive young guy, probably only a few years older than me, and he's worked here almost as long as I've been coming here. He told me his name once, but I missed it in his thick accent and never thought to ask him for it. It wouldn't be a problem if he wore his name tag, but he never has it pinned to his shirt in the morning when he starts his shift. I smile at him as he hands me my coffee and I hand him a five dollar bill. We have an unspoken contract between us, he has my coffee ready before I get to the front and he can keep my change. It's a good contract I think, keeps me out of the waiting line and gives me more time to people watch.

It's apart of a morning ritual I adopted because of my creative writing teacher last year. Once he took us to Tim's and told us to write about one unusual person in the restaurant. We had to detail their appearance, their mannerisms, and anything we noticed about them, then use them as a character for a story. I keep with it, writing in my people notebook. I never use anyone as characters, but I create stories for them. Give them interesting lives. Happy lives.

Sara, stop.

It's like recording birds or wild animals in their natural habitat, only with a lot more shouting and a lot less pooping in random places on the floor. It would be a lot more interesting if that would happen though. Knowing the way that some people act in public, I'm waiting for the day it does.

A man comes in the front door and catches my eye. I start writing about him.

> *Male, middle aged, balding. Black coffee, large cup. Breakfast sandwich. Probably business man, but he could very well be a prince in disguise from some obscure country. Maybe he's searching fo*

The next customer in line perks my interest more.

> *Female, PINK MOHAWK. Probably an Amazon warrior, super tall. Kind of intimidated by her but also feeling a little bit of butterflies? Or I'm getting sick from eating too many pancakes? Either way, 10/10. She's probably Wonder Woman's sassy lady side kick getting coffee for their kick ass adventures. I want hair like that. Wearing a leather jacket, so she probably eats men's hearts for breakfast. Awesome.*

My phone alarm starts to blare as I'm about to write about the next customer.

Go to school now Sara.

I scoop up my things and start to make my way out of the door, bumping the Pink Mohawk girl with my shoulder. I barely reach her waist with my head.

"Sorry bout that!" She says cheerfully. Her voice is incredibly high, like an anime character. I feel like I'm about to vomit out a swarm of butterflies. She's so pretty.

Calm down Sara. You're okay.

"My fault," I say, and practically run out the door.

> *Female, PINK MOHAWK. Probably an anime character.*

3

When I get to school the hallway is filled with chatter and cluttered with freshmen. They're like sheep; mindlessly wandering around in groups, always on the lookout for predators like the notorious Nathan Hill. I call him the pig man, because he's been uppercutted in fights so many times that where he once had a nose is now just a flat plain of nostrils. Not quite full Voldemort, but damn well getting there. He's sinister like Voldemort too, but not in a "kill Harry Potter" sort of way. I don't think his goal in life is to take over the world, just to ruin lives and be an asshole. He's very good at that, probably the only thing he is good at. He hasn't killed anyone, to my knowledge that is, but he is the grossest person in the senior class.

Nathan and the Queen Bee are two of a kind. Kindred spirits, maybe even twins in some weird alternate universe. They're both cruel dictators of high school, though Nathan only rules his four man troop of idiots and Queen Bee rules over everyone. They both take some kind of sick pleasure out of hurting others and out of hating people.

The only differences between the two are their genders, appearances and past selves. Ali is a pretty girl who once was nice, and Nathan is ugly as all hell and has never been anything but evil. I've heard rumours that when he came out of the womb he punched the doctor in the face, which sounds ridiculous until you meet him. He's the kind of guy who picks on you relentlessly for no reason at all, to the point you want to die. He's also the kind of guy who always wonders why he doesn't have a girlfriend, but to the girls in the school it's not a mystery.

Nathan has three principles in his love life that he actively follows:

1. If you're a girl and you don't want to touch his junk, you're a bitch.
2. If you're stupid enough to touch his junk, you're a dirty whore.
3. If you refuse him too much and he's been his definition of nice to you, he deserves to take you himself.

He's the big bad wolf that the freshmen sheep stare down the hallways in fear of. I've been lucky to avoid his sexual advances at least. Queen Bee made sure of that when she started her reign over everyone, and labelled me the school lesbian in a cruel twist of irony. I suppose I should thank her for that really; I'd rather have Nathan smash my head against a pole than smash his junk against my body.

As I open my locker, the chatter in the hallway goes quiet. Some girls giggle and gossip, and I know why they are. The whispers are always the same, laced with poison and accusations. They remind me of the buzzing of bees, which is appropriate considering the people who whisper about me serve the will of Queen Bee. The whole school is a hive, lacking the sweetness of honey and the sense of togetherness that bee hives have.

Calm down Sara, you'll be okay. Don't listen to it Sara.

"That's her," one of them says, and the other gawks at me.

Don't listen to them, ignore it.

"Did you hear about what she did in middle school?"

Oh god, I think. That shouldn't even be a thing anymore. But I know it will never stop being a thing because Queen Bee has told everyone. We all have labels, and Queen Bee is determined to keep it that way, and with every batch of freshmen the rumours fire up anew.

I slam my locker, and the girls shut up their giggling. I walk past them, head down, to get out of the hallway and to my first class.

You can't let this bother you. You can't. You have to be strong. Get over it.

I walk faster, because I can feel myself want to cry. I want to get out of here. I shouldn't have come to school.

I slam into someone and fall backwards, and when I look up I almost scream. I should not have come to school today.

"Watch where you're going, Super Dyke," she says. My heart stops. Queen Bee stands above me, her two drones laughing behind her. Behind her caked on makeup she looks unimpressed, almost angry.

Her name is Alison Parker. If she were a movie character she would be Regina George from Mean Girls, and her friends would be Gretchen and Karen. Their names are Miranda and Amy, and while they are both pretty and bitchy in their own right, they pale completely to Ali Parker. Ali is the bombshell blonde that pre-pubescent boys have wet dreams about. She's the tallest girl in our senior class, and has all the characteristics of a Barbie doll super model celebrity. I stare at her, taking in her Barbie doll appearance. Her long bottle blonde hair falls in perfect curls around her face, reaching down her back. She's wearing a dress today; white with pink polka dots that reaches just above her knees but long enough to pass dress code. Her legs are long and tanned, and she's wearing black flats on her tiny feet. My eyes jolt back up to her face. She has the prettiest face of anyone in the school, maybe even Hollywood. Her almond shaped brown eyes sit under her thick brown eyebrows. Her nose is long and pointed, and slightly pinker than the rest of her face excluding her plump lips. Freckles splash across her face like orange paint flicked off a paint brush. Everything about her looks painted on, especially the perfectly winged eyeliner that sits on her eyelids. In a word, everything about Ali Parker is perfect. Except for her personality. She looks like a doll, and when she opens her mouth I you almost always wish she was.

To put it nicely, she's a complete and total bitch. She makes Regina George look friendly.

Calm down, she's staring at you.

"Sorry," I say, and I scramble away from her as fast as I can. I can feel my sweat beading down my neck and my heart beating so fast it wants to give up. She doesn't say anything as I leave, but I can hear Miranda and Amy giggling like school girls until she starts walking down the hallway again. I turn to watch her go, and for a second I almost miss her.

No Sara, she's not the same person. Stop.

She used to be my best friend when we were younger. Before we got into middle school and she met Miranda. At the time she was my neighbour, and when we first met she marched up to me with a handful of worms. It was disgusting, but I liked her spunk. It was something I lacked in my childhood. Ali was once an outgoing girl whose hair was always cut short, and who had knees peppered with scratches and bruises. She always had Band-Aids on her face, and more often than not was missing a tooth. I had long red hair, a trait I inherited from my dad, and always wore dresses. We were exact opposites, but we became fast friends.

But, like all my friends, eventually she decided that our friendship had to end. Unlike my other friends, our friendship ended by her punching me in the face and calling me a slut. It was a while before she labelled me the Super Dyke, early in the summer. I went over to her house in the morning to hang out. When I got there, Miranda was there. I had known Miranda from school, because she was in my class and used to pick on me. Needless to say, I was unbelievably confused to see her at my best friend's house. I asked Ali if she wanted to hang out, but she was acting angry and distant. Then she suggested we go to the park, and when we got there Ali started yelling at me. Then she hit me and spat on me and . . .

She's not the same person anymore. Don't think about her anymore. Go to class.

4

I get to class early, and Mr. Lewis looks up from his coffee cup to give me a tired smile. He's a young teacher, probably the youngest in the school. Because of this he looks like he should be a student, not teaching them. He doesn't try very hard to look professional either, which doesn't help his appearance. He has bright and curly red hair that he never seems to be able to control, and thick rimmed glasses. He tries to grow a beard, but it makes him look like a hipster lumberjack because of his affinity for wearing plaid shirts and skinny jeans.

Mr. Lewis starts writing down questions for us to answer on The Great Gatsby, and my pencil follows his movements exactly. I'm not interested in the questions at all, in fact I could care less, but it feels good to move my hand. I've always felt calm in using my hands; doodling, scribbling, writing, fidgeting. My hands always need to be moving. I am a machine, my hands are my gears, without them moving I cannot function.

You need to function Sara.

"Can anyone tell me the theme of The Great Gatsby?" Mr. Lewis exclaims, expecting a sea of hands to crash into him like waves. He instead gets mumbles of I don't knows and shoulder shrugs. He sighs and starts to go off on one of his unending rants about literature that could teach you more about the book than the author could.

The Great Gatsby, from what I collected, is about the American Dream and the hollowness of people. It's about love and letting go. I found the biggest thing was letting go of the past. Past loves, past problems, past whatever's that trouble the mind. Gatsby had a problem with letting go of Daisy. I don't understand why he's so strung up on her, or anyone from his past. If I were him, I would be happy to let go of my past. I would love to rid myself of the girl from my past who toyed with me, the war I fought (though I'm still fighting mine, and there is a serious lack of Nazis; or an opposition besides the voices in my own head) and all the crap that Gatsby holds on to. You can't repeat the past.

Oh but you can Ol' Sport.

I feel like I've either been reading this book too much, or watching the movie with Leonardo Dicaprio that came out this year FAR too much. It's only November, so it has only been out about 6 months, but I've seen it enough to memorize every facial feature Leo managed to make.

That man deserves an Oscar, and every piece of underwear I own.

Mr. Lewis stops his rant to see if anyone is still listening to him. I nod at him, hoping he thinks I was. As much as I hate this class, I love Mr. Lewis and want to respect him. He's a cool guy; one of the only teachers who I feel actually cares about his student's well being. It might just be how he wants us to see him, but I like to believe someone cares about me.

People care about you Sara, don't put yourself down.

I stare at the clock and wonder how long it will be until class ends.

Tick tick tick tick tick tick, I follow the clock with my eyes.

Tock, something hits the back of my head. I turn around and see a crumpled piece of paper.

Tick tick tick tick tick tick, I keep thinking about the clock as I un-crumple it, and I'm getting nervous.

Don't look, throw it away.

Tock, I read it. I feel my heart drop to the floor and splatter. My blood goes cold.

'KILL YOURSELF SUPER DYKE, YOU'RE WORTHLESS'.

Ignore it Sara. You're not worthless.

You're worthless.

I swallow hard. I don't know who threw it, but the handwriting is crude so it's probably one of the low-lifes in the back with the same IQs as the crumpled paper they're throwing. I hear them snickering.

Ignore it, ignore it, you're worthless, ignore it. Class is almost over.

The bell rings and I get ready to join the rest of the students in the shuffle to our next classes. As I'm putting away my papers and books I can feel the unmistakable breaths of the pig man Nathan crawling down my neck.

Calm down Sara, you're worthless. Calm down.

I can hear him smacking his fat lips together. I have no idea why he's here. Maybe he'll finally get it over with and kill me. I probably wouldn't mind that, but I don't think Mr. Lewis would appreciate having to call the janitor to clean up my remains.

"Hey blotchy," he says, and I can't help but roll my eyes. Nathan started calling me blotchy in the 4ᵗʰ grade because of the port wine stain between my eyebrows and down the bridge of my nose. It's the least original insult anyone could ever come up with about it. I turn around to look at him. The first thing my eyes meet with is two big sets of nostrils staring into my eyes. Then I see the rest of him and I'm even more grossed out. He's recently cut his hair, making him look even uglier than before. His greasy mullet compliments his massive ears quite nicely, making him vaguely resemble a stereotypical hill billy. His friends are standing behind him, making a quartet of hicks. Their names are Gabriel, Joe and Cam. Of the group, I only like Gabe. He doesn't talk much, he doesn't bully anyone. But he stands by and watches, constantly frowning at his friends. He's really no better than them. I wish he'd speak up.

Nathan snorts when he breathes, and the disgusting sound snaps me out of my thoughts. I sigh and try to calm down my nerves. I don't like when he's so close to me.

"What do you want Nathan?" I say, trying to sound firm and unphased. I already know I don't.

Pig man brings his hand up and topples over my desk, scattering my books all over the floor. I can see Mr. Lewis staring, his brow scrunching together in an effort to look menacing. He looks more like a four year old than anything though; a black eye couldn't make him tough.

"Oh, sorry about that blotchy," Nathan laughs, and Joe and Cam copy his laughter. They sound like the pack of hyenas from The Lion King; stupid and clumsy, but lacking the wit and hilarity of Whoopi Goldberg. Gabe stares at me, his eyes concerned. I wish he was like my mom and could read minds.

"Mr. Hill, perhaps you could pick up Ms. Hale's books for her," Mr. Lewis says in a stern voice, if his voice could be stern. He sounds like an insecure puppy wailing at his owners to stop fighting and pay attention to him.

"I'm fine, I can do it myself," I say, barely audible.

You're fine Sara, you're worthless.

Mr. Lewis doesn't look convinced that I'm fine at all, and as Nathan and his pack walk away from me laughing he stands up from his chair. He goes to the door and closes it, telling any of his students who are in his class next to wait. I try not to look up at him as I collect my books but I can feel his eyes fixing themselves on me, waiting to start a conversation that I'll barely be apart of.

Finally I give in and look up at Mr. Lewis. His facial expression is the same one he always gives me, and I'm about 99% sure he's about to ask my why I put up with all the crap I do from Ali and Nathan. He asks me almost everyday when he sees it, but I see him do about as much as I do about it.

"Why do you put up with that?"

Why DO you put up with that, Sara?

"Well Mr. Lewis, it's either put up with it or be miserable and avoid coming to school everyday, so how about you choose which one I do or stop asking me about it."

"Sara, you can't let them treat you like that."

You can't let them treat you like that. You're worthless.

"Why don't you ever have this talk with them? Why is it always 'Sara don't let people treat you like shit' instead of 'Hey, don't treat Sara like shit'?"

Mr. Lewis sighs and rubs his head, tossing his red hair around and making it look like his head is on fire. It reminds me of Ghostrider, but a lot less Nicolas Cage in appearance and more Chucky from the Rugrats.

"Can I go now, please?" I say, my voice breaking a bit. Lewis nods and hands me a pink late slip with messy writing on it, which I'm sure he intends for me to give to my next teacher.

I leave the room and get swept up in the migration of the freshmen sheep. Some of them start whispering when they see me, but I run through the halls before I can catch enough of an earful to get upset about it.

You're worthless Sara. Get over it. Kill yourself. You're okay.

I decide to skip my next class, math, because I'm already considerably late and Mrs. Hunter will have my head. I've never been a model student in her class, and I can't stand her. Her constant droning on and on about math reminds me of the adults in Charlie Brown, even though she's excited about fractions. Who the hell gets excited over fractions? Crazy assholes, that's who. Mrs. Hunter is most definitely a crazy mathematical asshole.

Skipping class means one of three things to me; I either go home, to Tim's, or to the library. I figure it's too early to go home, and I've been to Tim's recently so it's not much of an option. The library is my best and most comfortable option. The librarian shushes anyone who talks too loud. If anyone is whispering about me, I won't be likely to hear it.

You're worthless. You're worthless.

The library in our school is kind of pathetic. It's small and smells like gym shorts and old computer dust, but the librarian is young and nice. She kind of looks like Mrs. Hunter, if Mrs. Hunter were a sane person. They both have the same straight hair and big nose, but they have different eyes. The librarian's eyes are soft and sweet. Mrs. Hunter's eyes look like the eyes of a mathematician crazed on an overdose of meth and denominators.

I find the first empty table I can and spread my books on it to discourage anyone sitting with me, even though the likelihood of anyone doing so is slim. People tend to stay away from me to avoid being the target of Queen Bee. It's social suicide to be seen with the super dyke, because everyone knows the worst thing in the world to be is not straight. If you're a complete bitch, you're still okay if you're straight.

People are incredibly stupid and I hate them.

The only person who has seemed to ignore the social suicide of being my friend is Colten, but even he's not that great about it. He's only here to continue getting into my pants when I'm sad and provide his miracle cure for my depression in the form of a relationship.

Then suddenly he's walking into the library, smiling and waving at me.

I figured he would come; he has an incredibly creepy way of finding me no matter where I go. My best guess is that he's got a tracker planted on me, though I have no idea how he would get it on me. Possibly one of the times I've been naked in his bed.

"Hey beautiful!" he says to me, grinning like an idiot child on Christmas. I try my best to look enthusiastic but I can't. The friendlier I am to him, the more he overestimates our friendship. I already screwed it up before by sleeping with him in my loneliest state of mind, but pleasantries make it worse.

Calm down Sara. He just wants to talk. Get over it Sara. You're worthless.

"Hey," I say, trying to not sound completely awkward. He takes a seat across from me and weaves his fingers together on the table top, leaning towards me.

"I thought I'd find you here. You should be in math, you little rebel," he laughs, trying to be flirtatious. I don't even make an effort to smile at him. I just shrug and raise the corners of my mouth enough to make him think I don't want him to leave.

"Yeah that's me. Total rebel."

"So I've been meaning to ask you . . . Are you going to the dance tonight? And if you are, do you want to accompany me?"

"Oh come on Colten, you know dancing is not my thing."

"Well, I thought you would like to get out of the house for a night. You never want to do anything fun with anyone."

"There's a reason for that Colten, I'm not a very big fan of fun."

Colten leans back. I can tell he's getting frustrated with me but I don't really care. I don't want to go to the dance.

Just try Sara. Just try. You're worthless.

"Colten, dances are for popular kids who have dates and want to experiment with drugs and sex."

"I'll be your date, and we can fuck and do coke after. Just let me take you out for one night. Please."

I stare into his eyes trying to stand my ground, but it's incredibly hard. Though I'm not romantically attracted to him, I can't deny his unbelievable charm that has girls fawning over him left and right. He's got lovely olive skin and gorgeous brown eyes, and his dark hair is always messy but in a sexy way. I realize that he's not taking no for an answer, and I sigh as loudly as I can to let him know I'm not impressed.

"Fine."

He smacks the table, eliciting a "SHUSH" from the librarian. I can't help but flinch at the sound of his hand hitting the wood. Colten stands up and leans over the table to kiss my forehead.

"I'll pick you up at 7," he says, and walks away from my table. I bite my lip as I watch him leave the library, and start thinking of ways to get out of going. Knowing Colten, I'd have to be on my death bed, which doesn't seem too bad, but I'm trying to avoid that. I'm stuck.

He's always been like this, even when we were younger. He practically begs and begs and begs until you cave in and do whatever it is he wants you to. That's how he got me to start hanging out with him all the time when we were younger, and how he got me to sleep with him when we were older. It's not that I don't like him. I just don't like him that much, and to him that's a problem because he can't stand being stuck in the fictional confinements of the friend-zone.

Just try to be normal Sara, you're worthless.

I look at the library clock. It's only 11, but I'm already fed up with school. If I leave for the day my parents will flip out, but I don't really have enough energy to care about that. I'm too tired. Exhausted socially even, despite having the minimal amount of social interaction that one can possibly have.

Get over it Sara, you're worthless.

5

I figure that because I've already skipped one class, there's no point in going to my next class. Instead, I leave the library and sneak out the front doors of the school.

The day is a little cool and foggy, and I breathe the chill in deeply. I start to walk away from the school, trying to decide where to go until 3.

Go back to class Sara.

A black truck starts to pull over beside me and I try not to freak out. They could be parking, or they could be trying to kidnap me, but either way I start to walk faster. It keeps creeping along beside me, and the passenger side window starts to roll down. I start walking even faster.

"Hey, Sara!"

I turn and look at the driver of the truck. Gabe waves at me and I look around to make sure he's not talking to some other girl named Sara. I raise my hand and shake it a little bit. He smiles and motions for me to come in his truck.

I'm uncomfortable.

"Hey, where you going?"

I shrug. Still uncomfortable.

"Well why don't we go for a coffee?"

I stare into the truck, nervous. Gabe laughs and looks behind him for a second.

"Don't worry, it's only me. No Nathan."

He smiles at me sincerely. I'm still hesitant to trust this guy.

Go Sara. Like the kids say; you only live once.

Yeah okay, but what if he has ill intentions, then what is your stupid saying good for?

I open the door and climb into Gabe's truck. The cab smells like mint and roses, and the seats are soft. Gabe smiles at me and pulls away from the sidewalk. I put on my seatbelt and breathe hard. I can't believe myself.

I'm an idiot. An idiot who gets in the truck of a boy who watches her get bullied.

"Is there anywhere specific you wanted to go?" Gabe asks and I shrug. Coffee means Tim's, and there are about 5 in town.

"Wherever," I say, because I don't give a damn which Tim's we go to. Gabe nods.

We drive past a Tim's and I stay quiet. The radio is playing something quietly, and I strain my ears to listen to it. Coldplay I think. I want to turn it up and drown out the awkwardness of the drive but I don't know how Gabe will react.

"So why did you pick me up?" I say, because I feel awkward and Coldplay isn't helping. I look at Gabe, and my throat tightens. His face is completely straight, and he bites his lower lip a little bit.

"I just . . . I just wanted to talk to you about them," he says, his voice getting lower as he talks.

"What?" I ask, swallowing. I feel like I can't breathe.

Gabe pulls into the parking lot of a Second Cup puts his truck into park. He looks at me with glassy eyes, and then reaches for my arm. I flinch away from him, and he stops. He reaches again, pulling up the sleeve of my bunny hug. I look away because I can't handle seeing them again.

Gabe puts his hand on my arm and rubs them. I look at him, feeling on the verge of tears.

"It's okay," he says. He pulls up the sleeves of his own shirt, revealing his own. I look back into his eyes, unsure what to say.

"We don't need to go for coffee. We can do drive thru and go out for a drive instead."

I nod. He pulls out of the parking lot.

6

I tighten my grip on the hot cup of tea in my hands. The burning feels good and makes me feel more comfortable as Gabe drives down the highway. We've been driving for half an hour, and I have no idea where we are; but I feel safe in the weirdest way.

Gabe turns on to a back road and I look at him. I try to build up the courage to talk again.

"Where are we going?" I say finally. Dirt and rocks splatter against the windshield as they fly up from the rough road. The truck hardly takes a hit from them. My own car would be destroyed by this road.

"To my favourite place in the world," he replies, and pulls off to the side of the road. I look out the window and nearly gasp at the world outside. Gabe gets out of the truck and walks around to open my door for me. When he does, I'm hit with air that smells like freshly cut grass, lake water and trees. I can see why it's Gabe's favourite place in the world. There is a huge body of water at the end of hill that seems to go on forever because of the way it mirrors the sky and trees all around. By the edge of the water are flowers and lily pads and all kind of other flora. Gabe walks down the hill and takes a seat on the grass. He turns and motions for me to follow.

"This place is amazing," I say. Gabe nods.

"Why did you start?" he asks. Right to the damn point.

I suck in air and look at the water.

"Well," I say, not sure exactly where to start. I begin by telling him about my friendship with Ali.

"My mom and dad had just moved here when I met her. We were originally from Saskatoon, but my mom was having an affair with one of the men she was working with at the public school she was teaching at. My dad wanted us to move somewhere where Jesus was more of a focus."

"He's in the wrong place," Gabe says, and I laugh.

"Well, Alberta is more old-fashioned than Saskatchewan in his mind. Anyways, we moved here. When I first met her I was outside our new house playing with our old dog Tina. She came right up to me and tapped on my shoulder with her grubby fingers. She was covered in mud and it got all over my dress. She asked me what my name was, and I told her. Then she told me her life story, then her name. She asked me if I wanted to see a dead body, which made me cry. Then she told me that there wasn't really a dead body at all, just a chalk outline of one of the boys on the block who she kicked in the balls. Then she invited me to make mud pies with her, and told me she liked me. And from that moment we were friends."

"Ali sounds like a weird kid."

"Yeah, she really was."

I keep going, telling Gabe about the summer when Colten moved to the block and Ali fell head over heels in love with him. I told him about our sleepovers where she talked endlessly into the night about Colten, and the days we would watch him from across the street while we giggled to ourselves and how I didn't understand why.

"She was my best friend, and she was always there for me. Like, when my neighbour Mr. Murphy, had molested me in the park by the elementary school, I cried in Ali's arms for days because I didn't know who else to go to. And she sat there with me, brushing my hair back and kissing my forehead as I cried and not one minute did she judge me."

Gabe shifts closer to me, putting his arm around me. I smile a little at him, and breathe deeply again because I can feel my eyes watering.

"We were so close, I felt myself falling in love with her. And for a while, I thought she was in love with me too. I asked her to be my valentine in grade 6 and she said yes. We played in the park until it was dark, building snow castles and snow angels. And as we sat in the castle we built I leaned in to kiss her, because I wanted to know for sure that she liked me back."

"And did she kiss you back?"

"You don't get to know that," I laugh, punching Gabe's arm. He laughs with me.

"Then she found out that Colten had a crush on me. He had brought flowers to my house, and she found them on my front porch before I did. As soon as I saw them, I wanted to throw them away and tell her I didn't like him, but she stormed off crying. She didn't talk to me for months, and when she finally did . . ."

"Well, she yelled and screamed at me and punched me. And when school started, she used everything she knew about me to torment me.

24

She's the reason people call me the Super Dyke in school. And that's why I started."

Gabe pulls me in for a long hug. His shirt smells like mint and musk and a thousand other smells. When I pull away I notice I've left tear stains on it, and that he's left tear stains on mine.

"Why did you start?" I ask him. He lays down on the grass, putting his hands behind his head. He sighs, and licks his lips. I decide to lay beside him, and he moves closer to me.

"Couple years ago my mom got sick. She had leukemia, and not one of us had the slightest idea until it was too late and she was lying on her death bed. My dad couldn't handle seeing her die, so he left me and my little sister with her. Still don't know where he went, but I know that he abandoned my mom. She died two days after he left, crying out for him because she had gotten delusional and didn't remember that he abandoned us. My little sister Molly and I were left with my grandparents. Molly and I wanted to stay and work on the farm, but my grandmother didn't want to move from Red Deer and my grandpa was too old. My uncle came and took over, and I made Molly go with our grandparents because I've never trusted my uncle. I just wanted to stay and keep my mom's farm for her, take care of her garden and her rabbits. My uncle worked me to the bone and would hit me when I disobeyed him, and it all built up until I couldn't take it anymore. So I started cutting, and it calmed me down when I was angry because I finally had that release I needed-you know what I mean?"

"Yeah," I say, unsure what else to say. Gabe sighs.

"It's an awful habit to have. I've only recently stopped."

"What made you stop?" I ask. I want him to say something that could help me too.

"I beat the shit out of my uncle the last time he laid hands on me. Knocked all his teeth out and demanded he leave."

"And he did?"

"No, he punched me back. And he kept hitting me until he passed out from exhaustion. And then I called the cops and got myself away from that."

"What about the farm?"

"I realized that my happiness is more important than the remnants of a dead person, and that my mother would have given anything for my safety; even the farm she loved so much."

I roll on to my side and look at Gabe. He looks back at me, and I can see tear stains streaked on his cheeks.

"We should go back," I say as quiet as the wind that is blowing around us, "I have to go home before it gets dark."

Gabe bites his bottom lip, but then he sits up. I stand before he does, wiping my body down to get all the grass off. Gabe stands up too, and pulls me into a hug.

"Sara, please stop hurting yourself. It's not worth it."

I bury my head into him and nod. As I pull away from the hug, Gabe grabs a hold of my hand. It feels different from when Colten does it. Safer, more welcoming.

We start walking back to the truck, still holding hands, and I realize that the voices in my head are quiet. As Gabe walks to the door of his truck, I can't help but wonder if he's the reason why.

"You'll save a dance for me later, right?" He asks.

I nod, almost too willingly, because I really want to dance with him.

7

I stare into the mirror and shift uncomfortably. The person in the mirror is an alien, someone I have never seen before. I know it's me; it just doesn't look like me at all. I'm wearing a strapless teal dress that stops just above the knee and black tights and shoes. My hair hasn't changed, I brushed it but that's the extent of style I could put into it. Short hair isn't very doable. I've put on a little bit of eyeliner and lipstick to doll myself up too, but I feel like I don't look good. I look too unfamiliar to look good.

Get over it Sara, you're worthless.

My mom comes into the bathroom and smiles, placing her hand over her mouth. I look at her eyes, and notice she's tearing up.

"You look so beautiful," She says, and I look back in the mirror. I smile, and I can see it for a second. It's fleeting, but it's there.

Get over it Sara, you look so beautiful.

I start to say something but I'm interrupted by a knock on the door. My mom smiles and holds up her camera to me, snapping a candid before running towards the stairs. I follow her, and see Colten already inside talking to my dad. When he sees me coming he smiles, and holds up a corsage to show me. I smile, but I'm not happy. It's not a date, we're going as friends. Maybe he didn't get the memo.

"Wow," he says, breathing long and hard, "You look amazing."

"Thanks, my dress has pockets," I say, and he puts the corsage on me. I fake a smile again, and Colten smiles back genuinely.

My parents keep us behind to take pictures. By the time we finally leave the house I'm already exhausted and want to go back in to sleep.

You look beautiful Sara.

We get to the school quickly and find a good parking spot close to the doors. I watch as all my classmates pile into the front doors, cheering excitedly until they reach the teachers tasked with frisking suspicious students and checking student ID. Colten opens the door for me, and quickly snatches up my hand before I can find a chance to run away.

"You ready?" He asks. I shrug, then nod, then wish I had shaken my head and made Colten take me home.

Just breathe. You're beautiful.

The gymnasium of the school is booming with loud music and the exhausted cheers of students awkwardly working out moves on the dance floor. The air is humid from the sweat and breath of the people cramped into the tiny gym space that's been created by a wall that cuts the usually large gym in half. I watch Colten dancing while I lean against one of the cold stone walls of the gym.

Dance with him Sara, you're worthless.

Colten looks at me and smiles. I give him a half smile, and he takes that as an invitation to come over and strike up a conversation with me.

You're supposed to be his date, this is what dates do idiot.

"Are you having fun?" he says between huffs of breath.

"Yeah," I lie. I want to go home.

Colten sighs and leans on the wall next to me. He puts his arm around me, and I flinch instinctively.

"Hey, it's okay," Colten tries reassuring me. He starts talking about something, but I tune out immediately because I can see Ali staring at me from across the room. She looks angry or annoyed or something but she's looking at me and I'm terrified. Colten stands up straight and grabs my hand, pulling me to the dance floor. As a slow song starts he pulls me into his chest and wraps his arms around me to dance. I keep looking at Ali, her gaze fixed on mine. She says something to Miranda and Amy, and they laugh.

"May I cut in?" I hear someone say, and I turn around to see Gabe. I look up at Colten. He looks annoyed, but he gives my hand to Gabe anyways and walks off to the wall to pout.

"How are you enjoying the dance?" Gabe asks. I shrug.

"I want to go home. I hate these kinds of things," I say. Gabe laughs.

"Then why did you agree to come? You shouldn't feel obligated to do the things you don't want to."

"Colten asked me to."

"You guys are . . .?" He asks, raising one of his eyebrows.

"No. Just friends," I say, and I look away from Gabe to look at Colten. He's staring at me, his face practically turning red.

"Maybe you should tell him that," Gabe laughs, and I stifle a laugh with him. The slow song ends and transitions into some upbeat song that makes me feel like I'm in a Fast and Furious film. Gabe lets go of my hand and I smile at him before going back towards the wall to see Colten.

"Hey Sara, why don't you come dance with me?" I hear from behind me, and my heart drops out of my chest and splats against the floor. I turn my head to see Ali with her hands propped on her hips, scrunching the fabric of her pale pink dress. She's smirking at me, and I know she can tell I'm afraid of what she has to say to me.

My body reacts before my mind does, and suddenly I'm running from her. I crash into the back doors of the gym, forcing them to fly open and hit whatever was behind them. The closest doors lead to the girl's bathroom, and I run into it at full speed. I find the furthest stall from the door, a handicapped stall, and lock myself in it. I climb on the toilet to hide my feet and wait. I grab my phone from the pocket of my dress and start to text Colten when I hear the door creak.

"Oh Sara? Sara are you in here?" Ali calls out into the bathroom, being replied only by the echo of her own voice. I gasp and cup my hands over the mouth in an attempt to reclaim the sound, but I can hear her laugh quietly to assure me she heard.

I hear her start kicking in the doors of the bathroom stalls, and panic starts to flood my chest and drown me.

"Come out, come out, wherever you are . . ." I hear either Amy or Miranda say. They both chuckle regardless as Ali's foot slams into my stall door. I hear her swear under her breathe, probably because she hurt herself being a bitch, and she starts slamming harder on the door. I feel like I'm in a horror movie, starring as a poor unfortunate girl about to get murdered by the serial killer.

"Please go away! Leave me alone!" I say, panicking as the lock begins to give out. I sound like a girl in a horror movie now. I scramble off the toilet and try to squirm under the wedge of space between stalls to make my escape. I hear the door break open and feel someone grabbing my foot. I kick at Ali, screaming as she pulls me out of the stall.

One thing I can compliment Ali on is her refusal to adhere to stereotypes. Girls usually rely on words and social status to bully others, but Ali likes to get physical. It's apart of what has made her so terrifying to other girls; if you do something she doesn't like, she will destroy your face and your social status.

I try to crawl away from her but my face meets Miranda's feet. Ali grabs my hair and forces me to sit up by pulling it. I can feel myself crying as my heart beats out of my chest. Ali leans down so that our faces meet and smiles.

"Hi Sara," she says. Her voice is sweet like honey but it makes my whole body shake violently.

"You know, I've been thinking a lot about you lately. Especially, about you and Colten."

"Why is that my problem?" I ask, grinding my teeth. She smiles again. It makes her even more terrifying, because she's not even angry. She's not hurting me out of spite, but out of enjoyment.

"Well, I was just thinking about how unfortunate it is that you two are so close. After all, we had such a great history together and you're well aware of how I feel about him. Aren't you?

I cringe. I don't like where this is going.

"It's just not fair, is it? That we can be friends but you treat me like this? No regard to my feelings at all."

I want to say something so bad, but I don't want to lose teeth.

"You can have him," I say, "Just let me go and leave me alone, please."

I sound pathetic, like someone begging for their life. I wouldn't put it past her to kill me though. She's a little bit of a psychopath.

"Oh, but that's not good enough. See, I don't like you Sara. And I know as long as you're around Colten isn't going to be looking at anyone else."

"Are you threatening to kill me? Because this isn't some crappy teen drama show you will actually go to jail for that."

"I'm not an idiot, Sara," she says.

Could've fooled me.

"I'm going to make sure he never looks at your pretty face again."

And suddenly she goes into a rage, throwing me to the ground. She begins to stomp on my torso and scream insults at me, calling me a slut and other disgusting names. I cry and scream and beg and apologize, desperate to get her off me every time her high heel slams into my skin. I can feel it puncture my chest, and I start to bleed. Every stomp winds me and I start coughing violently, choking up mouthfuls of blood and saliva. Finally, Miranda pulls her off.

"Why don't you do the world a favour Sara? Kill yourself you piece of shit," Ali says, making sure to get as close to my ear as possible. I whimper, and listen as their footsteps quiet as they walk out of the bathroom and down the hallways.

Why don't you do the world a favour Sara? Kill yourself you piece of shit.

I curl into a ball and cry. Maybe I should do just that.

8

I don't want to get up off the floor of the bathroom, but I have to force myself to. Every movement shoots pain through my body, and I clench my teeth to prevent winces from escaping my mouth. I try to balance myself with my hand, but I mistakenly place it in a puddle of my own spit, tears and blood and I slip. I crash back onto the floor of the bathroom, crying out in pain.

"Is someone in there?" a voice calls into the bathroom. I know immediately that it's Mr. Lewis because the voice squeaks. Lewis gets nervous when he's around girls and their bathrooms. I clamp my hand over my mouth because I don't want him to come in and see me like this. I know he'll demand to know who, and when he finds out it was Ali I'll never hear the end of it.

You should have stood up for yourself. Why do you let her treat you like that?

My voice betrays me, and I wince in pain again as I shift my body/

"Mr. Lewis," I call out, nearly crying. I try to recall my words but all I do is hack and cough and gasp for air. Mr. Lewis runs into the bathroom, nearly tripping over himself. He stares at me with a horrified look in his eyes.

"Holy shit," he whispers. I would laugh if my lungs wouldn't rip apart. He scrambles to grab paper towels, then scrambles even more to bring them to me. I sit up again, trying to hold myself together.

"Sara, are you alright?" he says, panic obvious in his voice.

Tell him what happened.

Kill yourself.

"Yeah, I just tripped," I lie. He obviously doesn't buy it. I wouldn't either.

"Sara, I'm going to go call an ambulance and we are going to get you to-"

31

"No, please don't!" I say, grabbing Mr. Lewis's jacket sleeve. I can see my blood soaking into it but I don't care. I can't let my parents find out about it, and going to the hospital will do just that. Then I have to deal with my dad getting upset that his "perfect family dynamic" is failing again.

"Sara, I-"

"Mr. Lewis *please*," I beg. He looks at me, concerned. Finally, he sighs and helps me up.

"I'll call the janitor to clean this up. Do you have a way to get home safely, Sara?"

I nod, even though I don't. The last thing I want is Colten to drive me home and make a big stink about Ali.

You're an idiot Sara, kill yourself.

Mr. Lewis leaves the bathroom, and I turn to the mirror to make myself look presentable. My face looks almost blue, and compared to the rest of the bathroom I look dark. I turn on the tap and splash cold water on my face, opening my mouth enough to catch droplets. It washes away the rusty taste of blood and cools my throat. I wash some of the water through my hair and over my eyes, smearing the makeup on my face.

I leave the bathroom, not bothering to fix myself up. I walk down the hallway of the exit door and push it open, straining my ribs with the weight. I feel like I might collapse from the pain, but I need to keep going. I need to go home.

"Sara?"

I turn and see Nathan, Gabe, Joe and Cam smoking with some of the other people from school. Gabe walks up to me, throwing his smoke on the ground and stepping on it. Behind him his friends snicker, and Nathan smiles like a devil from a cartoon. I step back for a moment, then look back at Gabe. I feel like I'm going to cry just seeing him with Nathan, because I know he's so much better and because I could cry anyways.

"You look pretty hot in that dress blotchy, didn't know you could look like that," Nathan sneers. Tears start escaping my eyes.

"Hey, shut the fuck up Nathan," Gabe says. Joe and Cam look at each other, confused. Then they look at Nathan.

"Whoa calm the fuck down Gabe, he was just giving the bitch a compliment," Joe says.

"I said, shut the fuck up. Don't talk about her like that or I'll beat your fucking face in."

I've never seen Gabe like this, and from the look on everyone's faces I'm not the only one. When he turns back to me, his face immediately loses all the anger that was in it when he spoke to his friends.

"Can you take me home?" I ask, my voice breaking into a whine. Gabe nods, and puts his arm around my shoulders as he walks me away. I can hear his friends snickering and calling out to us but I can't bother to listen to them. I don't want to listen to them.

Gabe's truck is parked in the teacher's parking lot, so the walk from the door isn't far. Still, he keeps his arm around me until we reach his truck. I can feel his body tensing up as we walk, and I feel as though he is ready to hurt anyone who tries to come close to me. When we get to his truck he opens the door for me and helps me in. I wince as I try to lift myself in the seat, and wince even more as he lifts me by my armpits. When I'm in, he goes to the driver's side and climbs in.

"What happened?" he asks once he's got his seat belt on.

"Ali," I reply, and he starts his truck.

The rest of the drive is quiet, and I don't know if it's because Gabe doesn't know what to say or he's afraid to say anything. When we make it to my house, he pulls in the driveway and looks at me.

"Are you okay?" he asks. I shake my head.

"Do you need me to come with you?" he asks. I shake my head again. He bites his bottom lip and hands me a piece of paper.

"If you need me at any time, call me. I don't care where you are or what time it is; call me."

I nod and look at him, on the brink of tears again. He leans towards me and pulls me in for an awkward front seat hug, obviously trying not to hurt me. When he pulls away he stops at my face, and we lock eyes for a second. Then he kisses my forehead, and moves his lips to my ear.

"Please, don't do it."

I get out of his truck and practically jog into the house.

Lou is on the step, howling like a lunatic to be let in. I let him in, closing the door quietly and tiptoeing up the stairs to prevent my parents from hearing me home. I look at the clock in the hallway. It's only 9 o'clock. I stayed at the dance for less than an hour. My parents are going to have a fit. Colten will have a worse fit.

I walk into a table at the top of the stairs, sending a violent surge of pain through my body. Before I can stop myself, I vomit in the hallway. I stumble away from the putrid stench and open the bathroom door.

I rip my bloodstained dress off, tossing it to the floor. I hear my cell phone clunk against the floor as it falls out of the pocket in my dress. I move to grab it, but I feel my stomach knot up again and I throw myself into the shower before I can make a bigger mess. I turn the water on the highest heat setting, and wait for it to warm up. As the heat starts to rise, I start to shake and cry. I watch as blood runs into the drain, and I look down at my body. My fingers feel along my ribs until I find it; a puncture in the skin on my ribs from Ali's high heel. I touch it, embracing the pain like an old friend. I unhook my strapless bra and pull my panties off, throwing them on the floor beside the tub into a wet mound of cloth.

Do it.

I rub my hands over my face, scrubbing away the makeup and tears from my cheeks.

Do it. Do it. Do it. Do it. Do it. Do it. Do it. Do it.

I open my mouth and drink the hot water and try not to think about it. My hands crawl along the wall of the shower until I find the soap holder.

Do it. Do it.

My hand grips the tiny thin handle of my shaving razor. I don't want to open my eyes.

Do it.

I open my eyes and stare at the blades. I run my finger along them, feeling it slice my skin. It's not deep enough to seriously harm me, I think to myself, I'll only cut once.

DO IT.

I bring the razor to my inner thigh and press down on it, dragging it horizontally across my skin. Tiny beads of blood start pooling from the two cuts the blades have made, and I breathe out as hard as I can. I do it again, and again and again and again until my fingers feel numb from pressing down so hard. I set the razor down in the soap holder again and move my hand to the fresh cuts, squeezing them as hard as I can. I close my eyes and let the shower run on my head until it starts to go cold, and by then I can't tell what part of the water is from the shower head and what came from my own eyes.

I get out of the shower and grab a towel, sinking to the floor of the bathroom. I see my phone vibrating on the floor and I reach to pick it up. I have 8 messages.

Colten Shepard, 9:15pm
Hey, where are you?
Colten Shepard, 9:30pm

Are you in the bathroom?????
Colten Shepard, 9:35pm
What the fuck Sara
Colten Shepard, 9:45pm
Cam said you left with Gabriel. WHAT THE FUCK
Colten Shepard, 9:47pm
seriously?? you are my date and you fucking leave with
another guy? WOW sara I can't fucking believe you
Colten Shepard, 9:48pm
here I thought you and I were fucking close like I do
so much for you and this is what I get??????
Colten Shepard, 10:00pm
Fuck you too you fucking whore
Colten Shepard, 11:00pm
im sorry

I try not to cry again as I read the messages. I expected this, I knew he'd be upset. I look over at the crumpled, bloodstained dress in the corner and grab it with my foot. I pull it towards myself and I stick my hands in the pockets to find Gabe's number. When I find it I type it into my phone and type him a message.

Me, 11:06pm
Gabe . . . I'm so sorry. I had to do it.

9

I wake up on the bathroom floor to the sound of Lou scratching on the door. I look at my phone to check the time. 8am, which means I'll likely be late for school. Having a dance on Thursday is the stupidest idea our school board has ever come up with apart from dress code. I try to stand up but my body aches all over, from Alison going to town on me, me going to town on myself, and from the weird position I was sleeping in. I look in the mirror and I look like hell. My hair is messy, my face is puffy and I look paler than I should.

I need a sick day. I need to stay home.

Get over yourself Sara. Kill yourself.

I walk out of the bathroom and Lou rubs against my leg. He meows at me, and starts purring. Lou has a weird way of sensing people's feelings I think. There must be some sort of sadness detector in his infinite fat rolls.

"Sara? Is that you?" I hear my mom call from downstairs. Damn Lou, alerting her to my presence. I clear my throat and prepare to make the worst sick voice I possibly can so she will let me stay home. If she gets a look at me she will let me stay. Or more likely, she'll take me to the hospital and scream at me.

"Mom, I feel sick. I'm going to go back to bed, okay?" I say, trying to sound as raspy as possible. I don't give her time to say anything else, I just walk into my room and crawl into my bed. I can smell bounty sheets, meaning my mom changed my sheets while I was out last night. My bedding feels good on my body; cool and soft and everything I need. My eyelids start to get heavy, and I drift asleep.

I wake up to my phone vibrating. Gabe's name is on the screen, and it takes me a second to register that he's calling me. I swipe the screen to answer it.

"Hello?"

"Oh thank god you picked up. I was worried after your text last night and how you weren't answering my texts this morning. Where are you?"

"I'm at home. I didn't want to come to school."

I can hear him take a long breath.

"It's a good thing you didn't."

"Why? What's up?"

"Miranda and Amy put up a video on Facebook last night. Everyone's seen it."

I try to stop the sound from falling out of my mouth by covering it with my hand. He can't be talking about the bathroom. He can't be.

"Why didn't you tell me Ali did that to you?"

Oh my god. Oh my god.

Get over it Sara.

I don't remember seeing any cameras or phones when we were in the bathroom, though my focus wasn't on whether I was being filmed or not.

"Are you sure everyone has seen it?" I ask, dreading the answer.

"You're the talk of the town, and not in a good way. The whole school was looking for you. Colten especially."

"He must be pissed."

"At us especially. He thinks you should have gone to him after. He also thinks we slept together and he wants to kick the shit out of me."

"Oh god."

"Yeah. Are you doing okay?"

"Well I'm embarrassed, I have a puncture wound on my side, my neck hurts from sleeping against the bathtub, it hurts to walk because I cut my thighs and frankly I could die and it would be a relief."

"Well I'm going to try to prevent that last bit. Do you want me to come over? We can watch a movie or something and I can bring over five tubs of your favourite ice cream."

I laugh a little bit. Gabe laughs with me.

"Yeah okay. I hope you like Doctor Who."

"Who?"

"Exactly," I say and hang up. I look at my phone and frown. Colten has messaged me again.

Colten Shepard, 8:02am
Where are you?????
Colten Shepard, 9:00am
Talk to me babe . . .
Colten Shepard, 9:05am
I'm sorry. I'm an idiot. I saw the vid. Wish you
would have come to me tho . . .

Colten Shepard, 12:05pm
Hey.

I delete his messages. I don't need his drama right now. My phone vibrates again, but instead of Colten it's Gabe.

Gabe Davidson, 12:10pm
Be there at 3:30. Gives you some me-time.
Don't start Dr. What without me.
Me, 12:11pm
Doctor Who.
Gabe Davidson, 12:12pm
Yeah, him too. See you at 3:30!

By the time Gabe knocks on the door I look less like a complete train wreck. Rather than deal with my wild hair I just tucked it away under a toque, and put on shorts and a tank top. I look relaxed, maybe a little tired, but good. If my mom sees me, she'll think I'm sick but not hospital sick.

When I open the door for Gabe, I see that he wasn't kidding about 5 tubs of ice cream.

"You like Neapolitan right? If not I've got chocolate, strawberry and vanilla separated. And cotton candy, just in case you want to feel especially happy inside," he says, laughing. For once, he's not wearing his farming hat and I can really see his face. He reminds me a lot of Roger from 101 Dalmatians, mostly because his nose is so big and dorky. But it's cute, and makes him look good. I also see his hair colour for the first time, and to my lack of surprise he's a blonde. His skin is dark, but something tells me it's just because of his farmer's tan.

"Are you going to let me in or just stare at me all day? I know I'm sexy, but control yourself," he says and I laugh. It's an honest and full laugh, something I haven't had in ages.

I help Gabe carry the stupid amount of ice cream to the basement, and put it in the freezer that my dad had installed in our laundry room. When I get back to the loft in our basement Gabe has sprawled himself on the couch, and Lou is laying on top of him in roughly the same position.

"I'm just going to go grab us some spoons, and maybe a lint roller for you. Lou sheds like a monster."

"He's so fat. Why is he so fat? What do you feed this guy?" Gabe asks, before breaking into Phoebe's smelly cat song from friends. Lou meows every time Gabe looks at him, and I can't help but laugh at how ridiculous they look.

I run upstairs and grab spoons as fast as possible. When I come back downstairs Gabe is smooching Lou's head.

"You like cats, huh?"

"Oh man. Love 'em. They're like little baby lions filled with pure malice and stupidity."

"Sounds like Lou alright. So, since you've never seen Doctor Who before and I don't want to go back to the beginning of the show we will start with Nine."

"Nine what?"

"Nine the doctor. You'll get it in a bit," I say, and turn on Netflix.

We spend a few hours watching Doctor Who and working our way through the Neapolitan ice cream. Then Gabe turns to me.

"Sara?"

"Yeah?"

"What are you going to do on Monday, when you have to go back?" he asks, his eyes full of worry. I shrug my shoulders.

"What I always do, I suppose. Grin and bear it. If not, bear it and hide my frown."

"Do you get tired of it? I know I did."

I sigh and look at Gabe. My body feels heavy.

"I've been tired since the day I became the laughingstock of the school. I've never stopped being tired."

Gabe stays quiet for a moment.

"It'll get better you know."

"Maybe," I say, but I don't believe myself at all.

10

On Saturday morning I wake up on the couch with Gabe. He's sleeping with his head on my lap, his slow breathing the only thing I can hear in the house. For a moment I panic, knowing my parents are probably home and they've probably noticed me downstairs with a boy; but the slow breaths of Gabe calm me down. If they had noticed, they won't say anything until he's gone.

Gabe stirs and then looks up at me with sleepy eyes. I smile at him, and he smiles back. His smile is crooked but genuine. It makes me happy.

"Good morning," he says, yawning as he talks.

"Morning," I say, and Gabe gets up off my lap. I'm almost upset about it. He was keeping my warm.

"What time is it?"

"No idea. Early enough that my parents are probably home."

"Oh awesome," he says with sarcasm. I nod and roll my eyes. I'm going to be in the deepest dog shit in western Canada when Gabe is gone.

"Should I go?" he asks, and I nod again. The longer he stays, the angrier my dad will be when he yells at me. Gabe gets up and grabs his coat from the chair, and I stand up and stretch.

When we get upstairs my parents are waiting in the kitchen. My dad is sitting at the table, holding a cup of coffee in on hand with the other one clenched into a fist. My mom looks at me, sympathetic. They're preparing for a game of Good Parent Bad Parent, and I can already see which role is being filled by who.

"Good morning Sara. Mind introducing us to your friend?" my dad asks. His teeth are clenched, meaning he's trying to be civil until Gabe leaves.

"Hello sir, my name is Gabriel Davidson. I go to school with your daughter."

"Nice to meet you Gabriel. Are you on your way out?"

I want to say something to my dad about being rude but I don't want to make him any angrier than he already is. Gabe nods and goes to the door. He puts on his shoes and looks back at me.

"See you later Sara."

"Bye Gabe," I say, and he leaves. As soon as the door closes I can feel the tension in the air.

"Take a seat, Sara."

I take a seat across from my dad. He's in his late 40's, but like my mom he looks quite young. His hairline is beginning to recede, making his red hair look like it wants to escape his head. I stare at it, afraid to look him in the eyes.

"We aren't even going to talk about you breaking the 'no boys after 9' rule," he starts. I'm surprised. Pleasantly, but surprised.

"We found blood in the upstairs bathroom, Sara."

My heart stops. I thought I had cleaned everything up. I open my mouth to defend myself but I can't form words.

"I-I'm on my period," I finally say. My parents don't look convinced. My mom sits beside my dad, entwining her hand in his balled fist. He moves away from her touch, and she recedes back into herself. They haven't been as close since the affair, and I feel like they never will.

"Sara, we aren't stupid. We know you're doing it again."

I bite my lip and look down. My dad sighs a loud, over-exaggerated sigh.

"Do we really have to go through this again? This is getting ridiculous Sara. We have spent a lot of time and money trying to get you better and every single time you go back to this."

"I know."

"Then why aren't you trying to help yourself? If this is your way of getting our attention, you're doing it wrong."

I nod because I don't know what else I'm supposed to say. They always think I'm trying to get attention or that I'm faking it for something. When someone is convinced, it's hard to change their mindset and my parents are beyond convinced.

"I'm going back to bed," I say, standing up. My dad grunts in frustration.

"I'm not done talking to you young lady."

"I'm done talking to you."

My dad starts to yell, and I ignore him as I go upstairs. I close my bedroom door and listen to them fighting. I always seem to be the reason they fight. Sometimes I feel like if I didn't exist they would be happier. My mom would have left my dad a long time ago if I wasn't in the picture, and my dad would have found a new wife with perfect children. Instead they live here, miserable with the worst marriage and child anyone could have. I am the catalyst to their misery.

I close my eyes and start falling asleep to their shouting. I dream of Gabe's spot, and me being there happy. Alone except for a few deer that graze on the flowers there. The sky is pink and warm, and the water is quiet and clear.

My phone blowing up with buzzing is what wakes me up. I have 2 missed calls from Colten, 18 messages from Colten, and 80 missed notifications on Facebook. Curious, I open up the app. First I think it's a malfunction, until I see my wall. People from school have posted the video to my wall, followed by hate messages and memes based off my profile pictures. I click on the video and it takes me to the YouTube where it was posted. It's gone viral with over a million hits. Over a million people mocking me. Suddenly Facebook buzzes again and I'm bombarded with inboxes from countless people, some I've never met before, insulting me. I start getting texts from random numbers with the same hate messages. I nearly toss my phone across the room, screaming because I don't know what else to do.

Lou pushes his way into my room and jumps on the bed. I scoop him up and hold him close to my face. His fur catches my tears as I start to cry, and I bury myself further into him. He starts purring loudly, and I can feel the vibration of his raspy purr on my cheeks. He starts to squirm in my arms, and I let him go. I collapse onto my bed and stare at the ceiling. Lou wraps himself around my head and starts licking my hair. I close my eyes in an attempt to stop my tears from overflowing but it doesn't work. I let out a loud sob and rub my eyes.

"God Lou, what am I going to do? Everyone hates me."

You deserve it. Kill yourself, you're worthless.

Lou keeps purring, licking faster and harder in some effort to make me feel better. Lou has always been a better parent than my own, who are too caught up in themselves and their image to see me crumbling at my foundation. Lou has always focused on me. I am Lou's world.

I try to think of what I should do, but only one thing comes to my mind.

Kill yourself.

Shower. I'm going to take a shower.

11

I don't want to wake up today. I know what's going to happen the moment I walk in the doors of the school. I can already hear the whispers floating inside my head, laughing at me.

Did you see the video Sara? You deserved it. Kill yourself.

I skip the shower today because I showered yesterday and the temptation to cut again is overwhelming. The old cuts on my leg are itching like crazy and the new ones on my shoulders are still painful from being fresh. I try to get my hair into some kind of order, but it decides on its own that cowlicks are in today. I shrug at myself in the mirror. I already know that today is going to be shit. This can't ruin my day further than it will be ruined when I get to school.

My phone vibrates in my bunny hug pocket and I pull it out. Among the countless notifications from Facebook and my inbox, there is a new message.

Colten Shepard, 7:30am
I'm here to pick you up. We need to talk.

Oh for fuck sakes. Awesome.

I go downstairs, hoping to grab some breakfast but he's already in the doorway.

"Hey," I say. He looks angry and unimpressed. I know he's going to demand answers for questions that he doesn't need to be asking as soon as his eyes meet mine. He walks out the door without saying anything. My mom is standing in the kitchen. I look at her and shrug, because I know that she's confused. Colten is usually friendly with her, trying to win her favour in hopes she'll arrange our marriage or something.

I follow Colten outside and climb into the passenger side. He starts driving, and I can feel the heat and tension filling the car. I'm suffocating in it.

You deserve it. Kill yourself.

"You haven't answered any of my texts or calls all weekend," Colten says. I breathe in and bite my lip.

"First you ditch me at the dance, then you get the shit kicked out of you and instead of coming to me you go to that shit face Gabe. Then when I try to talk to you, you ignore me. What the fuck Sara?"

What the fuck Sara? Kill yourself.

"I'm sorry I didn't realize that Ali beating me up in the girl's bathroom was my fault," I say, sounding more sarcastic than I intended to. Colten grunts.

"You should have come to me. You were at the dance with me, you were my date. You're not Gabe's girlfriend Sara," he says through gritted teeth. I can't believe him.

"I never said I was. He's my friend."

"Friend? This is the same fucking guy who stands there when Nathan picks on you. When the fuck has he ever stood up for you?"

"When have you? You're never around when ANYONE is picking on me. You're so focused on getting in my pants that you don't even see how shitty everyone treats me. You focus on Ali and Nathan because they're the fucking super villains and you need to look like you actually give a flying fuck about me but you don't. Ali cares more about me than you do," I say the last sentence louder than I intended to, but I mean it.

"What do you mean I don't give a fuck?! I'm the only one who has ever been there for you, and even then you won't fucking open up to me for one minute. I try so hard to make sure you aren't alone in this because I love you. I'm trying my best to help you get rid of this, let me help you," Colten shouts. Rage starts to boil inside of me. He always has to be the victim. He's the victim; he's always the forsaken one.

"You think that you're the cure for the way I feel about myself Colten? You think you can remedy this just because you love me?"

"You don't know until you let me try. You've never given me the chance to prove to you that-"

"No Colten, you know what? I'd rather be alone than have you around at this point. Your friendship does nothing except hurt me because I'd rather not commit to you romantically."

"You sure seemed to commit to me when you were spreading your legs for me not too long ago!" he screams. My heart stops for a moment. Slut shaming is beyond classy and far beyond what I'm willing to put up with from Colten right now.

"Colten, that wasn't commitment. That was me feeling lonely and you being desperate enough to ask me to have sex with you. It was nothing," I try to say calmly, but I say it through clenched teeth.

"Has all this been nothing to you? All these fucking years of friendship have been nothing to you?"

"No Colten, they've just been more to you than what they should have been."

Colten stops the car outside the school doors. I climb out of his car, still fuming.

"Fuck you Sara."

I turn to say something to him but he speeds off before I can think of anything clever.

My head races violently as I push open the heavy front doors of the school. The loud chatter in the hallway stops almost immediately when I walk in. I can feel everyone's eyes staring at me, and as I start to walk down the hallway I can hear the whispers.

Ignore it Sara. Kill yourself.

When I get to my locker, I see that someone has written "FUCKING LOSER" on it with permanent marker in messy handwriting. I try to ignore it and I open my locker, but I'm painfully aware that it's there. I look around at the freshmen sheep, which suddenly look more like wolves. They lick their chops with hunger and malice, whispering my name in hushed voices laced with venom. I swallow hard and slam my locker. The whispers fly away like packs of birds, the only whisper left cawing in the hallway my own.

Kill yourself.

I walk down the hallway, looking around for Gabe. He's the only person I can talk to anymore. He's the only person who doesn't hate me to my core. Years ago that would have been Ali.

But she's not the same anymore. She's become the leader of the wolf pack in the halls that started the first rip in my flesh and ignited the feeding frenzy on my body. And despite all of that I really wish I could run to her right now. I wish I could curl up on her lap like I did when I was a kid and have her brush my hair back. I wish she were the Ali I let myself open up to countless times in the still nights when she would stay over, her breathing in tune to mine and her fingers entwined with mine. I miss the friend I had.

Then I see her and I remind myself who she is. As she walks past me in the hallway with a glare and a smirk I remind myself that she killed the girl who loved me. She killed the girl that I loved, and it's likely that she will kill me too.

12

Class is easier than the halls. Everyone is expected to be quiet as Mr. Mickler rambles about chemistry and makes obscure Breaking Bad references so the whispers stop for a while. The way Mickler acts, it's almost like he actually emulates the show as much as he idolizes it. He shakes his hands violently when he says the words "elements", "science", and "methamphetamine", making the class laugh. I tune out and stare at the posters on the walls. The classroom reminds me of an elementary school, if an elementary school were run by AMC. There's a Clifford poster beside a poster of Walter White in his underwear, and I try to picture what would happen if we were in an elementary school.

Mickler would likely be arrested, I'd probably be happier in general, and I wouldn't have to hear the group of girls behind me giggling amongst each other as they talk about me.

"Charlotte, I see you have a something to share," Mickler suddenly says, and I turn to look at Charlotte. She's a tiny girl with pink hair and dark skin that she covers with every makeup product available. She looks at me, and I look at the tiny folded piece of paper in her hands.

"Would you mind sharing what you and your friends have been so giddy about since class started? I'm sure we are all itching to read the story in your hands," Mickler says, motioning for Charlotte to come to the front. She shakes her head a few times, before reluctantly walking to the front of the class.

"Well, go on Charlotte. Read the note."

Charlotte locks eyes with me for a minute and I can see that she's panicking. Then I realize why.

It's about you. It's about you.

I suck in air as Mickler grabs the paper from Charlotte's hands. He starts reading it and his face drops. When he looks up at me, it confirms the contents on the paper. I can feel myself tearing up, and I feel like I've been punched in the gut. I don't even bother to pick up my stuff, I just stand up and walk out.

"Sara!" I hear Mickler call, but I slam the door behind me and start running. I can't stop the tears from flowing out of my eyes and the husky sobs from exploding out of my chest. Some people walking in the hallway look at me and laugh, but I keep going.

I don't want to be here. I don't want to be here. I want to die.

Then do it.

I run into the first bathroom I see. To my relief, it's empty. I pass by the mirrors and go to the last stall of the bathroom. I sit on the toilet and pull my feet up on the seat, pressing my legs on my chest. The walls of the stall are littered with graffiti, and as I read it my eyes sting.

Sara Hale is a fat loser
Sara Hale is a bitch
Sara Hale = S L U T
I fucking hate her
I hope she kills herself
    YEAH
       Me too . . .

I cross my arms over my knees and bury my face in them. I feel like I can't escape it. I can't escape myself and the hate everyone seems to have built up for me. I want to scream, but all I can manage are sobs and hiccups and sore lungs. My body wants to hurt me too.

"Hello?"

I look up for a moment. I didn't hear anyone enter the bathroom because of my own sobs. I stop breathing, dead silent.

"Are you okay?"

I bite my bottom lip and sink my face back into my arms. I want her to go away, but instead I hear her sit in the stall beside me. I look over and see her shoes and realize they are Ali's favourite kitten heels. I can't hear anyone else, Miranda and Amy are usually laughing away with each other. She's alone.

"No," I say, trying to disguise my voice. I don't want her to know it's me. I don't want her to know I'm alone in the bathroom and completely at her mercy.

She stays silent for a little while, and I hold my breath the whole time. A knot is forming in my chest, forcing me to suck in a small breath. She sighs.

"Hey look . . . I know it may not mean much but whatever you're going through will pass. I mean, life kind of sucks all the time for all of us. Look at Sara Hale. She's going through hell."

"But that's because of you," I say, my voice cracking a bit. I hear her chuckle a bit. Fucking bitch.

"Yeah, that's true. But if she can handle that, you can handle whatever you're going through."

"Why do you hate her so much?" I ask on an impulse. I want to recall the words the second I say them.

Ali sighs again and I see her feet disappear. She's probably sitting on the toilet like me.

"I don't even know anymore. It used to be because of like, a boy, but now that's not even it."

"That's not what you said in the bathroom," I say, almost too fast, "I watched the video," I add to not be suspicious.

"Yeah I know. That was mostly to keep up appearances I guess. My friends still think I'm hopeless over that guy but I could care less. He's kind of a dick anyways. Not like I'm not a dick sometimes."

"So you just hate her because you can?"

"Yeah," she says, her voice trailing off.

"Her life is hell because of you."

"Oh I could care less," her voice trails off again and I hear her sniffle. I want to punch the walls in. I want to expose myself to her, but I'm afraid to.

"I—Why are you so upset?" she asks after a pause. I stand up and unlock the door.

"You," I say, my voice falling into a sob. I start running out of the bathroom, and I can hear her behind me for a second. I turn to look at her one last time, and our eyes meet. Her eyes are wide with confusion and worry, and she looks down at my arms. I realize that my sleeves are rolled up, exposing all the scars on my lower arms. She looks back in my eyes and starts to say something, but I run before she can.

The bell rings and people start filing out of their classes, cluttering the halls. I push through, the whispers starting up again. I head towards the front doors, determined to get out.

I slam into someone and I get thrown back a bit. Miranda turns around and looks at me.

"Look who it is, Amy! We missed you Sara!" she says, laughing. Amy laughs behind her. The group of girls they're standing with all look at me and start giggling. I try to walk past, but Miranda pushes my back.

"Where do you think you're going? We want to have a word with you."

"Leave me alone," I say, and I try to walk past again. She pushes me back again.

"I don't think so."

I push her, knocking her into Amy. They both fall on their asses, and the girls they are with all go quiet.

"Oh you bitch!" Miranda screams. I start running, practically bursting through the front door. My heart is racing violently, and I'm sure for a minute it's about to give out.

Please give out. Please give out.

I see Gabe standing with Nathan and Joe by his truck. He's got a cigarette in one hand, the other twirling the keys in the air on his index finger. I run up to him.

"Can you give me a ride home?" I ask, sounding frantic and breathless. Gabe looks at me, then at Nathan.

"Uh, I'm kind of busy right now. Can you wait a bit?"

"No I need to go. Now," I say, looking behind me. I feel like Miranda or Ali are stalking me like cats. I'm going to get pounced on before I can even escape.

"I would but I really can't."

"He's got prior obligations blotchy, now fuck off," Nathan says, and he takes a long drag of his smoke. I look at Gabe before I start running again. I feel a little betrayed. So much for the "there whenever you need me" bullshit. I should have known that when it all boils down to it I am alone. His friends are more important than me. Everyone is.

I'm alone and I don't matter to anyone.

13

When I get home the house is empty. Only Lou is home, curled up on the couch sleeping. I walk upstairs and into my room, slamming the door behind me. I sink down and lean my back against it.

Kill yourself. You're worthless. Get over it. Kill yourself. You're worthless. Get over it. Kill yourself. You're worthless. Get over it. Kill yourself. You're worthless. Get over it. Kill yourself. You're worthless. Get over it. Kill yourself. You're worthless. Get over it. Kill yourself. You're worthless. Get over it. Kill yourself. You're worthless. Get over it. Kill yourself. You're worthless. Get over it. Kill yourself. You're worthless. Get over it. Kill yourself. You're worthless. Get over it. Kill yourself. You're worthless.

I look up and breathe out hard. I want to rip my lungs out and throw them against the walls. I want to stop breathing and never breathe again.

Kill yourself. You're worthless. Get it over with. Kill yourself. You're worthless. Get it over with. Kill yourself. You're worthless. Get it over with.

I stand up and go to my bedside table. Inside is the journal I used to keep, a battered old thing with a cartoon unicorn on the front. Taped to the inside of the front cover is a picture of me and Ali when we were kids, holding a pair of dolls we made of each other. I start flipping through the journal because I can't stand to look at it. I don't want to look at her, but I mostly don't want to look at me. I've changed so much from the happy girl in the photo. There are no remnants of her or of the girl she called her best friend. Both of them have been gone for a long time. Even the me that I am now is gone.

I flip to the next empty page in the journal and grab the sparkly pencil in the drawer. I sharpen it with its matching pencil sharpener and start writing.

I write everything I can think of. Every word to describe how I feel and how I've felt for a long time comes flowing out of me. I feel like ripping the paper in half and swallowing it, even as my stomach churns. I write everything, and it disgusts me.

By the time I put the pencil down, I want to vomit. I also feel exhausted and emotionally drained. I stare at the pages of my journal. They are the last chapter of my life, and it's weird. It's weird writing something and knowing that the next person who reads it won't be you. It will be someone who is in the absence of you. Someone who knew who you were but never really knew you or saw how you felt. I write at the top "to the oblivious reader of my last chapter", and close the journal. I put the journal and the pencil back into my bedside table, but keep the pencil sharpener clenched in my hand.

Then I leave my room and head to the bathroom.

14

This is it.

I'm done. I can't handle this anymore.

As I work on getting the blade out of the pencil sharpener, I try to list off the people who will forgive me for doing this in my head.

Kill yourself. You're worthless. Get it over with. Kill yourself. You're worthless. Get it over with. Kill yourself. You're worthless. Get over it. Kill yourself. You're worthless. Get it over with. Kill yourself. You're worthless. Get it over with. Kill yourself. You're worthless. Get it over with. Kill yourself. You're worthless. Get it over with. Kill yourself. You're worthless. Get it over with. Kill yourself. You're worthless. Get it over with. Kill yourself. You're worthless. Get it over with. Kill yourself. You're worthless. Get it over with.

Kill yourself.

My mother won't, she always told me this was the coward's way out. I'm a coward though, I can't handle being "brave" anymore.

I suppose my dad will be there for my mother. She'll be a wreck. He will forgive me when his sadness recedes, he's a forgiving person.

Colten won't, but he's young. He'll get over it. He'll forget about me one day, when his life has formed new stories for him to write and maps for him to follow. I don't care if he never forgives me; I can't forgive him.

Gabe? Gabe doesn't know me well enough to care. He too will move on and never look back at me.

Everyone else will celebrate this because they won. They finally won and they broke me.

Kill yourself. Kill yourself. Kill yourself. Kill yourself. Kill yourself. Kill yourself. Kill yourself. Kill yourself. Kill yourself. Kill yourself. Kill yourself. Kill yourself.

God?

Of course God will forgive me, that's His job.

Though, I don't think I'll forgive God.

I bring the blade up vertically on my left arm. I'm stronger with my right hand, and I pierce deeper than I thought I could. The pain feels so good to me, I feel so alive. I am full of butterflies, erupting inside of my chest like a swarm of hungry predators.

And why would I forgive God? What the hell has God done for me lately? Turned my best friend into my relentless hunter, fucked my ability to have relationships. Fucked me over completely; what the hell kind of God does that? An asshole does that. Sunday school never told me God was an asshole. All those years with my dad telling me about God, and not one mention of how much of a dick he can be. They should consider rewriting how they teach the bible to kids.

"God drowned a lot of people, told a guy to kill his son AND fucked Sara Hale's life over so he's an asshole, now let's pray."

Something tells me that's not going to go well with the devout Christian parents, but the truth never has.

I take the blade between the fingers of my left hand, and stare at my right arm. I twist the blade, and I can feel the sweet edges cut eternities into my skin. My hand is weak from blood loss but that won't matter soon. I put the edge of the blade against my skin and hold it there, pressing it down into me. Into everything I am; everything I was. I am at the end.

What about Ali? I don't even know why I'm thinking about her but I am. Will she celebrate my death too? Will she be happy that she finally broke me, and that someone that she hates is finally gone and that she'll never have to look at me again? I desperately wish she was the Ali from my childhood. That Ali would cry and try to stop me. She'd tell me not to do it.

But that Ali is dead. She's as dead as I am.

Do it. Do it. Do it. Do it. Do it. Do it. Do it. Do it. Do it. Do it. Do it. Keep going.

My heart starts racing and I hesitate.

Fuck Sara, you can't chicken out now, you're so close.

I'm so close to being far away from Ali Parker and every moment of torture she gave you. I'm so close to never having to walk down that hallway, that stupid green mile where they whisper about you, ever again. I'm so close to freedom.

Just do it.

I drag the blade down slowly, pushing it in deeper as I go down the length of my arm. My hand starts to shake as the blade meets the end of my wrist.

Fuck.

It feels so good.

I drop the blade on the floor and let my arms leak out my existence on the tile floor. The world around me is going blurry, except for the brightness of the bathroom bulbs burning into my face. I stare at them until my vision goes black.

15

"Hello?" I say, and my voice echoes in the bathroom. Whoever was crying stops, and the room goes dead silent. I start walking towards the last stall, but stop when I hear her breathe out.

"Are you okay?"

I look at my phone to check the time. My bathroom break has already been more than 5 minutes, which means that Mrs. Hunter will soon come looking for me. The woman can't have one person be out of class or she'll explode, but I have to piss like a racehorse and I can't with some chick crying. I go in the stall beside the girl and sit on the toilet. It feels really weird sitting on it with my pants on.

"No," she finally says. Her voice sounds familiar, but it falters as she holds back a sob. I sigh, unsure of what to say or do. It's not often I'm expected to comfort someone. The only person I've ever been friends with who I've had to comfort was Sara. Miranda and Amy hardly need it. I'm a bit rusty, and the pressing matter of my bladder makes it worse. There's an awkward silence between us, and I look at my nails. I need to repaint them.

"Hey look . . . I know it may not mean much but whatever you're going through will pass. I mean, life kind of sucks all the time for all of us. Look at Sara Hale. She's going through hell," I say. The girl in the stall clears her throat quietly.

"But that's because of you," she says, her voice cracking. I chuckle a little bit.

"Yeah, that's true. But if she can handle that, you can handle whatever you're going through."

"Why do you hate her so much?" she asks. I'm taken aback by her sudden question. It's not something people ask me. People just know that I hate Sara and accept it because at this point everyone hates her too.

I sigh and pull my knees up to my chest.

"I don't even know anymore. It used to be because of like, a boy, but now that's not even it."

"That's not what you said in the bathroom, I watched the video,"

"Yeah I know. That was mostly to keep up appearances I guess. My friends still think I'm hopeless over that guy but I could care less. He's kind of a dick anyways. Not like I'm not a dick sometimes."

Sometimes is really an understatement on my part.

"So you just hate her because you can?"

"Yeah," I say, my voice trailing off. I think about it for a moment. I just hate her because I hate her. It's been such a long time that I have no other feelings about it.

"Her life is hell because of you," she says. I shrug, even though I know she can't see it. My bladder starts hurting and I shift uncomfortably on the seat.

"Oh I could care less," I say. I close my eyes and lean my head back. I really just want this chick to leave the bathroom so I can pee. I don't know what else to say to her, but I know if I don't go to the bathroom soon I'll probably die of some nasty piss disease. Disgusting.

"Why are you so upset?" I ask, trying not to think about pee. If I make her upset enough to talk about it she might leave, and that's really all I want right now. The girl gets out of the bathroom stall.

"You," she says, her voice falling into a sob. I nearly fly out of the stall. It was Sara, of course it was her. She's standing by the door to the bathroom, and I take a step towards her. The last time we were in the bathroom together I beat the crap out of her, and this time I feel like I've done the same thing 100 times over. She turns to look at me, and our eyes meet. I stare into her eyes, and my eyes travel down to her arms. Her sleeves are rolled up, and I realize that her arm is covered in blue gashes and bruises. Tiny uniform lines, freshly cut into her skin. I look back at her face, shocked. She has a black eye, rather blue eye, and tiny blue cuts in her face too. Then she runs from me, and I want to follow her and ask about them but I can't move. My feet feel plastered to the floor, and my whole body feels 100 pounds heavier.

Holy shit I'm going to fucking piss myself.

Finally I feel like I can walk again, and I leave the bathroom. I see Miranda stomping down the hallway towards me, pissed out of her tree. She moves her straight black hair out of her face and focuses her brown eyes on me.

"You won't fucking believe what Sara just did," Miranda huffs. Amy soon joins us, looking at her phone. She's trying to fix her hair, but like always it continues to look completely stupid.

"What?" I say, my tone harsh. Miranda sinks down into herself a bit. She's used to me sounding fed up with her, but it still always hurts her a little bit. She tries to pretend like I can't see it, even though she knows that I can.

"She pushed her into me," Amy says. I hate the way her voice sounds. She ends all her sentences like a question and makes her sound like her IQ is lower than it already is.

"So? Get over it," I say. Miranda looks at me like I'm a ghost. I guess she expected me to want to go after Sara, but I really don't care about whatever personal offenses she commits against Miranda. That and I don't even want to bother her. Whatever weird thing she did to herself to make her turn blue; I don't want to know.

I start to feel sick to my stomach thinking about it. For a moment my eyes go weird, and I see a flash of red on Miranda's face. I look around, and for a single moment everyone has red on their skin. I rub my eyes. I'm imagining things.

"Are you okay?" Amy asks. I shake my head.

"No. I'm going to go home, I don't feel well. Get my homework from Lewis."

Miranda nods and she and Amy leave. I fish my keys out of my pockets and head to the front doors. When I get outside I see Nathan and his friends leaning against a truck near my jeep.

"Hey Ali!" Nathan calls. I wave at him, but it's not a welcoming one. It's a dismissal, because frankly I hate Nathan and everything about him. Dude is a complete jerk.

"Ali what did you do to that freak Sara? She ran past here crying and asking Gabe to drive her home."

I shrug and look at Nathan's friend Gabe. He's a real cutie, but too much of a farm boy and definitely not my type. He looks at me with a hardened expression. For a moment he looks like he might have a black eye but when I look again I can see that he doesn't.

"You're friends with Sara?" I ask him. I thought the only friend she had was Colten.

"No," he says, looking down, "I was nice to her once and now she won't leave me alone."

"Oh," I say, and climb into my jeep. I want to play music, but when I turn it up my head throbs so my drive home is long and quiet. I pass by

Sara's house on the way, and for a moment I wonder if I shouldn't go over and see if she's alright.

But I also don't really care. That freak can die for all I care.

When I get home the door is unlocked, meaning my brother Ben is home. It's not a surprise at all. Ben spends his days playing League of Warcraft or whatever and making money off of art commissions. He's been graduated for almost 6 years and hasn't left the house since the day he got his diploma. As I pass by his room I can hear his speakers booming with fruity fantasy game music. Luckily, my room is mostly soundproof and when I close the door the fantasy crap disappears.

I lay down on my bed and rub my temples, desperate for relief from the wrongness I'm feeling in my body. It spreads all over me, and my hands start hurting. I look at them, and I can see blue cuts on my knuckles when I blink. Whatever this is, I can sleep it off.

I fall asleep.

16

I get up from my bed and stretch, my bones cracking as my limbs extend. I strip down into my underwear and stride towards the bathroom down the hall from my room. It's quiet in the hallway for once, meaning that Ben had decided to turn off his computer sometime in the night and sleep instead of levelling up his cleric; or whatever the hell he does on that stupid game he always plays.

I open the bathroom door and turn on the light. My eyes take a moment to adjust to the flash of light, and when they do I turn towards the mirror of the bathroom.

My first reaction is to scream.

It looks like someone had cut me while I slept; tiny scrapes and bruises covered my hands and stomach. My scar from having my appendix removed has reopened and as I lift my arms I could see that my elbows are scraped. My knuckles are peppered with tiny cuts and bruises and the palm of my left hand has a giant gash in it. Worse, rather than being red, my wounds are a vibrant electric blue and glowing. I scream louder.

Am I poisoned? Maybe I'm still asleep.

Maybe I'm having some sick nightmare.

I pinch my skin as hard as I can. I am awake.

"What the fuck."

I turn to the voice to see Ben. He's leaning against the doorframe of the bathroom, his shoulders relaxed and his legs crossed. Even though we live in the same house Ben never really leaves his room, and in the soft light of the bathroom he looks almost unfamiliar. It suddenly occurs to me why; I can see the bruises on his face clearly. Around his nose are massive bruises, seeping up to below his eyes like lakes connected by thick river. His neck is covered in hickies, bite marks and fingerprints. I stare at him, astonished. Not only because of the marks spread across his body, but also because he has hickeys, and I've never seen him leave the house.

Ben looks at me like I'm a stranger too, as if I were some deranged animal that got loose in his bathroom.

"Jesus Ali it's 8am. Can you tone down the volume?"

"Ben I-I'm freaking out. You're covered in bruises and cuts and-and I'm covered in them and they're *glowing*," I say frantically. I try pressing down on the cuts, but I don't feel any pain. I move close to Ben and press on one of the bruises on his nose. He moves back.

"What the hell are you doing kid? Fuck you're weird," he says, walking away from the bathroom and back to his room. I look back in the mirror and examine myself.

I feel much better than I did yesterday, but I look so much worse. I splash cold water on my face and start chewing on my lower lip. I stop. I can't go back to my nervous habit I need to calm down.

I try to get ready avoiding the mirror, which means no makeup and putting my hair in a ponytail. It's not something I usually do but I'm desperate. I put on jeans and a t-shirt and head out, not bothering to eat. I've lost my appetite for now, but I'll probably end up having a big lunch anyways so I can go without.

When I get to school something feels wrong. People are walking slower, and some people are leaving the school crying. I park and climb out of my jeep, watching them. One girl nearly collapses into tears as she goes to the car waiting for her. I notice the flag is at half mass, and my stomach drops.

Someone from the school has died and from the looks of it, it must be a student.

When I get to the front doors I throw them open frantically, and push through the groups of crying students in search of Miranda. As much as I dislike her at times, she's the go-to person for gossip and current events. I find her waiting outside my locker. Unlike the rest of the people in school, she looks completely unfazed. Amy too looks like she does any other day, but I notice both of them are covered in cuts and bruises too. They aren't blue like mine, but they're noticeably fresh. I take a moment to look around and see that all the crying faces around me have cuts or bruises on them. It's like overnight everyone joined Fight Club and beat the hell out of each other.

I walk up to Miranda and she gawks at me. It's the first time she's ever seen me without makeup or my hair done. It doesn't matter, I'm still prettier than her.

"You look like hell. Too sick to do your makeup or have you gone soft and been crying like everyone else has?" she says, picking her nails.

"Yeah I was going to ask you about that. What the hell happened? Someone died?"

"Wow, you didn't hear about it yet? Sara Hale died last night."

My heart stops. I look at Miranda and Amy in disbelief. Miranda said it so nonchalantly that it can't be real. No one talks about death like it's nothing.

"What?"

"Yeah. Apparently she killed herself in the bathroom. Cut both of her wrists right open. Her mom found her when she got home and she had already died."

I feel my mouth fall open. Miranda looks at me weird, like I shouldn't be reacting this way. I put my hand over my mouth, feeling a cough coming on.

"Poor Mrs. Hale . . ." I choke out. I try to breathe but it feels too short. Miranda shrugs.

"Whatever. I didn't like her anyways. No one did until they found out she died," she says, and she and Amy walk away. I don't follow. I don't want to follow.

I look around at the sobbing kids around me and suddenly I feel angry. Miranda was right, for once, when she said no one liked Sara. We all treated her like she was the scum of the earth, and yet here these people are mourning over her. Then I realize I am one of those people. If anything I should be more like Miranda.

The speaker for the announcements squeals.

"Attention students; there will be grief counselling in the library starting at 10 am. Today will be early dismissal; school will be ending at noon. Buses will not be running until 3 pm as usual, so please have a ride arranged if possible."

I contemplate for a moment going to grief counselling, but I realize that it's a stupid idea. I'm not grieving. She wasn't even my friend anymore, I hated her. You can't grieve over someone you hate.

Instead I turn and walk down the hallway in the direction of my class. I'm being ridiculous. I never cared about Sara Hale.

17

Mr. Lewis is quiet the entire class. Usually he's so energetic and excited about literature, but today he lingers around the class with a solid face. I watch him with concern, a stark contrast to the usual reason I watch him; because he's incredibly hot. He's hot without the massive bruise on his face that wasn't there yesterday. Everyone was better looking yesterday than they are today. I look around the class at my classmates. It's a flock of faces splattered with ugly purple bruises and nasty red scratches.

"Something distracting you, Ms. Parker?" Mr. Lewis asks. I shake my head. His voice sounds distant, weird compared to his usual overpowering presence in the class.

I look at the clock and frown. It's already 11, meaning I'm stuck in school for another hour. Another shitty hour of utter silence as the people around me pretend to be shaken up about the death of a girl no one cared about.

It's weird what a death can do to a school. Everyone becomes a child in the face of the death or a child, unable to control their feelings or their tears. I don't know if it's because people think about themselves being dead at a young age, or mourn the loss over a life so young. Whatever it is, it doesn't sit right in the chest to watch everyone acting like this.

The bell rings, and I'm the first to stand up and gather my things. Everyone else just sits there, their mouths straight lines and their eyes staring at the tops of their desks. Then they all stand up, not looking at each other or at me. I'm used to people avoiding eye contact with me out of fear, but not avoiding each other.

As I walk into the hallway it gets even worse. Usually the halls are clogged with freshmen chatting away but today everyone walks slowly and quietly. I watch them, their faces struck with black eyes and scratches. I rub my eyes, trying to get rid of the weird red spots in my vision that manifest on their bodies. It doesn't help. Everyone looks injured and it's pissing me off.

"Parker!" I hear someone spitting my name from across the hall. I turn and see Colten stomping down the hallway. He looks beat up too, and I can see hickeys all over his neck.

"Hey Colten," I say, unsure really of what to say. Colten usually barks some shitty insult at me when I pass him in the hallways. It's kind of pathetic really, and I've always known that he only did because he never protected Sara from me. He would tell her he "stood up for her" after calling me a bitch under his breath and she'd eat it up like candy. Personally I thought she was stupid for ever thinking he stood up for her. I thought he was even more stupid for thinking that I didn't know why he acted like that. I've got eyes and ears all over this school, and most of them belong to Miranda.

Suddenly I'm lying on the floor, my face throbbing. I look up and Colten is towering over me, his hand balled into a fist. Everyone around us is silent, and it takes a second for me to register what just happened.

"You fucking bitch! You couldn't stop until you had everything, could you! You had to kill her to be happy!" he screams. I don't know what to say back, so I lay there with my mouth gaped open like an idiot. A circle of people surround us, and I hear some people running away. Silently I hope they're running to get a teacher or something.

"You kept pushing her and pushing her off the edge until she jumped off! You killed Sara, you murderer! You murderer!" he screams louder, kicking me. I take it and don't fight back. He can keep hitting me all he wants.

"MURDERER!" I can hear his throat getting raw as he screams and slams his foot into me. Then he stops and I look up again, starting to tear up when I see the teachers pulling Colten away from me. One of the younger teachers, Ms. Belle, comes to comfort me. She's a pretty thing, straight out of college. I break into hysterical crying against her, throwing myself into her chest and grabbing her blouse for support.

"Ali are you okay?" she asks, genuinely concerned. I cry so hard I can't form words. Colten keeps screaming, but as they pull him down the hallway he gets harder to understand.

"Do you want to go to the nurse?" Ms. Belle asks. I shake my head and hug her. If I play this right she'll let me skip her class and I can go home before lunch even starts.

"Ms. Belle . . . can I go home?" I ask, and I try to sound as whiny and hurt as possible. She looks at me, furrowing her brow. Then she nods and helps me up. She starts to help me walk towards the stairs but I dismiss her by shaking my hands and smiling gently. I can tell she feels a little awkward about the whole situation, and she gives me a grateful nod before heading back to her class. As I walk down the stairs and towards the front door I can't help but smirk.

18

"Oh Sara? Sara are you in here?" I call out into the girl's bathroom, being replied only by the echo of my own voice. I wait a moment, and hear a faint gasp and the sound of hands cupping over the mouth in an attempt to reclaim the sound. I smile and motion for Miranda to watch the bathroom door.

Amy moves towards the sink and sits on top of it, ready to chase after Sara should she try to escape. I begin to kick in the stalls, calling out Sara's name with every swinging door.

"You can't hide for long Sara, we know you're in here! Come out, come out wherever you are . . ."

I kick in the handicapped stall at the end of the bathroom. Sara is curled up on the toilet, hiding her legs in her sweater; face down into her arms that are folded above her knees. She look up at me, tears rolling down her cheeks, smearing the makeup that had once graced her eyelashes and eyelids.

"Please . . . Leave me alone, I don't want this," She whispers. Her voice is cracking. I smile at her and grab her shoulder, feeling her flinch under my touch.

"Oh come on now, I just want to talk to you!"

"Please just stop!" She is begging now, and I can hear the terror rising in her voice. Amy chuckles behind me, and I grab Sara's arm. I pull her out of the stall, and as she falls forward her arm breaks off in my hand and bursts into maggots. Her blood splashes against my face and the walls of the bathroom, painting us a sickly blue colour. I look for Miranda and Amy, frantic for help, but they are gone. The room starts to fill with Sara's blue blood. I open my mouth to scream but the blood creeps into my throat and engulfs my lungs.

I shoot up from the couch, throwing my bowl of popcorn on the living room floor. The living room as dark, the only light being the TV screen as it replays the title screen for Sixteen Candles. I strain my eyes to look at the clock on the wall.

2:36AM.

I fall back on to the couch, exhaling. My t-shirt sticks to my skin using cold sweat as adhesive. I try to back track the hours from when I fell asleep to now. I felt like I was asleep for hours. I felt like I was awake the whole time too. I felt like it was days ago, until the dream went sour.

I fell asleep halfway through the movie, at midnight. 2 hours. 2 hours that felt like 24. Fuck.

I run my hand through my hair and sigh, closing my eyes. I want to sleep, but I can't will myself to. Instead I get up and drag myself to the upstairs bathroom.

I pull my clothes off and stare at myself in the mirror. I have large blue bruises where Colten punched me, making most of my body coloured blue. Blue, blue, blue; everything about my skin looks blue. Even the freckles on my face are covered by the blotches of blue. I trace my hands over my body, pressing each blue bruise as I go. Only the fresh ones hurt me, the others feel like skin. I frown and close my eyes.

I have no idea what's happening to me. I don't know why I see these things, but for the first time since I was little I feel scared. I feel like I'm going crazy.

I open my eyes and turn on the shower as hot as it will go, crawling in wearing my underwear. The water scalds my skin, and I hope to myself it will melt away the blueness that has become me.

19

I wake up to cold water raining down on me. I panic for a moment, then realize I'm still in the shower. Someone slams on the door, and I wait.

"ALISON, YOU'VE BEEN IN THERE FOR HOURS. GET THE FUCK OUT, YOU'RE WASTING WATER," my mom screams. She's probably drunk or high, or some combination of the two. I sit up and stretch in the tub, my body aching from the cramped space, and turn the water off. My skin is wrinkled and feels bloated with water, but for a moment I can't see the disgusting blue hue that it's adopted. I smile and stand up, thinking I've won.

I see the mirror and my heart shatters. My whole skin erupts into a muted blue glow and the bruises return, brighter than ever. I have to bite my tongue to hold back the scream that threatens to rip through my throat.

I don't know if it's from the shock or from the soreness in my legs, but regardless I fall backwards into the wall.

I force my body up again and leave the bathroom before I can look at myself again. I leave a trail of water behind me as I make my way to my room, knowing my mother will probably rip my head off for it. I can't be bothered by her anger right now. Something is wrong with me.

That hits me like a ton of bricks. I am never not okay. This is bullshit.

I straighten my posture and start rummaging through my closet looking for something to wear. I find the nicest, most expensive dress I own and put it on. It's a tight red thing that makes me look curvy, a stark contrast to my gangly boyish figure. It makes me look hot, but most importantly it makes me look put together.

I face the mirror, ignoring the blueness of my skin, and put on eyeliner and lip gloss. I take extra time with my hair, then move back and stare at myself. I look good—blue, but good.

I smile because I look like me.

"Allison!"

I break my thoughts when I hear my mother calling me. I take a deep breath and leave my room to go downstairs and face her.

She's sitting on the couch, slumped over like a crumpled mess of paper. Her skin looks translucent and sickly, and I can smell vodka wafting around in the air surrounding her. I crinkle my nose in disgust. She's been like this since the day my dad left, with no sign of it changing. He left her because of her drug problem, and she didn't get the memo that she should probably stop. For god knows what reason, he left me and Ben here too, and because of that Ben can't stand him. I forgive my dad though. I always will.

"Mom," I say gently. She turns to look at me but her gaze is lifeless. She goes through it a lot; anger and unpredictability and then suddenly she's lifeless like a zombie. I've always been afraid of turning into her.

"I'm going to school now," I almost whisper. She turns away from me again and I force myself out the door before she becomes enraged again.

By the time I get to school I'm feeling rattled and uncomfortable and I don't know why. There's an icky feeling deep underneath my skin that I try to fight off but it won't subside. I sit in my jeep watching the front door of the school. The people going in look like zombies, shuffling as if they've been drained of all energy. I roll my eyes. The death of Sara can't really be effecting them all like this. She didn't matter to them, or to anyone. The only person she mattered to was Colten, and even then she only mattered to him because she spread her legs for him.

The bell for first classes rings, but I don't get out of the car. I can't will myself to get out. I don't want to go in there. Seeing people pretending to care makes me sick, and the nasty bruise on my face is aching.

I put my jeep into drive and leave the front of the school. I need to clear my head, and I need to find somewhere to do it.

20

I pull into the parking lot of an old church close to the school. It's a brooding place, but on Wednesdays it's usually quiet and unoccupied except for care takers and religious nuts.

The outside of the church looks ancient, and is a stark contrast to its interior. Inside the church is vibrant and new, even though it still has that nasty candle and old people smell. I scrunch my nose and walk around in the front hall, unsure of where to go. The walls are decorated with children's drawings and old paintings of Jesus and other biblical shit that I don't care about. I don't remember why I wanted to come here until I walk into the incredibly quiet sanctuary.

I walk down the ugly mahogany coloured carpet until I reach the middle of the sanctuary. I sit on one of the uncomfortable wooden pews and sigh, taking in the room. The ceilings are high and decorated with poorly done paintings of angels, but the stain glass is beautiful. Light filters through it, making the room look like a vibrant rainbow. If it didn't smell so bad, and the crucified Jesus at the front of the room didn't look like the scream painting; I might think this place was relaxing.

"Jesus looks a little morbid, huh?" a voice behind me says. I turn around, slightly annoyed that I'm not alone and someone has the nerve to talk to me. Gabe is sitting in the final pew in the row opposite of mine, leaning back with his hands behind his head and his feet up.

"What are you doing here?" I ask, trying to sound harsh. I want him to leave, and leave me alone.

"I'm here for the same reason as you are. To confess my sins to screaming Jesus and be redeemed, all that shit. Maybe take a nap in the pews, exorcise my inner demons. You know, Christian things."

"I'm not here for any of those reasons."

"Oh? Then are you here for the funeral? Because if that's why, you're about two days early and in the wrong colour. You're not supposed to wear red at a funeral."

I feel my throat tighten.

"Why would you think I'd come here for that?" I ask, again trying to sound harsh but my voice betrays me and sounds small.

"People like us don't come here unless we're looking for answers or we feel like shit about our sins," he answers cooly. I shift in the pew.

"I didn't sin," I say.

"No one likes to own up to it, but we do it," he says back, getting up from the pew and walking towards me. I turn back to face screaming Jesus in an attempt to ignore Gabe, but he walks in front of my face. I look up at him and see the bruises on his face, the bruises around his neck, and the cuts on his shoulders that fall all the way down to his arms. I take in a deep breath, trying to hide my shock. I'm horrified, but I also note the absence of blue.

I want to ask him about the bruises on his body, but as I begin to speak he walks away from me and I lose my nerve.

"Friday at 4:30pm is the funeral, if you want to come. Don't know if she'd want you there considering all that happened, but maybe if you apologize she'll be okay with it."

"Apologize?" I ask, too quiet for him to hear me. Finally I'm left alone in the church.

Apologize? Bullshit. You can't apologize to the dead.

21

When school ends on Friday I almost run to the car, desperate to get away from the building. I feel like I'm in a school for the catatonic. The only people who seem to be responsive are Amy, Miranda and Nathan, none of which are good company.

I look at the clock in the dashboard of my car and bite my bottom lip. One hour. If I want to go I have to make up my mind before the hour is up.

I don't want to go. I know I don't want to go. The idea of cramping into a church full of sobbing teenagers pretending they knew a dead person sickens me as much as the idea of me doing it myself. No one cared about Sara. I didn't care about Sara.

My phone chirps at me and breaks my thoughts. I fish it out of my purse and look at the message on my screen.

Gabe Davidson has invited you to join **Sara Hale Memorial Page**

I click on it to look at the page. It has over 500 likes, with messages of condolences from my classmates.

We'll miss you Sara Xx
Love you so much Sara
RIP
RIP miss u

I keep scrolling and reading, feeling the bile in my stomach rise to my throat. They're all attention seeking idiots. Until she died, nobody cared.

I throw my phone into the passenger seat and start driving towards home. I don't want to go to her funeral, and I definitely don't want to be like them.

When I get home my mom is sleeping on the couch half naked. I can't smell booze in the air for once, but I'm careful not to wake her as I go past. I hardly make a sound until I get to my room and close the door, sighing when I do.

I grab my phone again and go back to the memorial page. There's an album of pictures on it, and a status update that says the time of the funeral. I click on the photo album and flip through it. Most of the pictures are school photos, where her mouth is in a straight line and her eyes are glossed over. Some photos are yearbook snapshots of school events where she's standing in the background, unsmiling and unengaged. I sit on my bed and flip through all of them, hundreds upon hundreds of pictures of the same sad girl, until I reach the last one. I nearly drop my phone when I look at it.

The picture is of two little girls smiling with toothless grins. One has messy red curls and a pink dress, and the other has cropped blonde hair, overalls, and about a hundred freckles. They're holding dolls of each other, complete with the Band-Aid on the blonde girl's face. They look like the happiest kids on the face of the Earth. They look like Sara and Alison.

At first I feel angry and embarrassed, and I wonder who in their right mind chose this photo. It's the last photo of us before we grew apart. Before I grew away from her. Before I became someone else.

Then I feel a great loss.

I look at the time on the top of my phone screen. It's 4:25, and the church is a 5 minute drive.

I get up and leave my room, grabbing the keys to my jeep and waking my mother in the process.

"Alison? Where are you going?" she asks, groggy.

"Out," is all I say, and I close the door. I don't have time to argue with her.

I get to the church only a few minutes late, but long enough that the service has already started. The pews are full, save for the last 4 rows. I grab a spot on the last pew and look around. Many people from the school are here; teachers and students alike, mostly crying or with solemn faces as Sara's father talks about her life and reads her tuning out for most of the eulogy, mostly because of the lies. Mr. Hale acts as if he and Helena have it all together, even though they don't. Worse, he acts like Sara had it all together.

It seems like forever until the funeral ends, and I hide my face under the hood of my sweater until most of the people have left. When I look up, that's when I notice it.

At the front of the church, under the feet of screaming Jesus, is her open casket. My body reacts before my brain can, pulling me towards the front in the same zombified shuffle everyone else has had since Tuesday.

71

I have to force myself to look at her face, and when I do look down all I can see is blue. Her lips are blue, her hair is blue, and the bruises and cuts on her skin are blue. She's glowing with the sickly electric blue that she was the last day I saw her. She looks like a corpse. She is a corpse, with blue cuts shining through the fabric of the dress that covers her arms.

"Man, the coroner did a good job. She doesn't even look dead," Miranda says, joining me. I look at her, confused. Then I look at the bruises on her arms, some of them blue, and I get it. I'm the only one who can see them. I'm not spared the make-up and fabric that hides the dead from the living as softens the blow of looking at them. I'm forced to see the truth of it, and the truth of everyone's bodies.

"What are you doing here Miranda, you hated her," I ask, trying to escape my thoughts about the bruises.

"Same reason you're here. To pay my respects."

"You've never been a respectful person."

"Neither have you, and you're here."

"She was my friend when we were younger."

"WAS. Past tense. This is the present, and I don't know about you but I have no time for the past," Miranda says, chuckling. She takes out a cigarette and puts it in her mouth.

"You can't smoke in here," one of the men in suits says. Miranda rolls her eyes and takes the cigarette out of her mouth, tucking it in the space between her ear and her head.

"We'll go outside then. Come on Ali, you look like you could use one of these bad boys."

I nod and follow Miranda out of the church.

22

"What do you think of all this?" I ask Miranda as she inhales the smoke of her cigarette. I put mine between my lips and ignite the end, sucking in the nicotine. It burns my tongue and lungs but it calms my nerves enough that my hand stops shaking.

"About you smoking? You only smoke when you're stressed out, so I'm thinking you're stressed out."

"No, about how people have been acting about Sara dying."

"I don't give a shit. You're all just acting like this because you're all 12 and you've never seen anyone die before. None of you knew her or cared about her so you all just look stupid," she says, exhaling. I look at her, confused.

"What do you mean 'you all'?"

"Oh come on Ali. The person who's been acting the weirdest about Sara dying is you. You haven't been the same since I told you. You've been acting like a fucking psycho. You're the one who started bullying her in the first place so I don't understand why you're so upset about it. She was fucked in the head, we should have seen it coming."

"I haven't been acting weird. I just . . . Something weird is going on with me."

"Yeah, it's called grief dipshit. You've been nice to everyone because you're afraid someone else will kill themselves or some shit, I don't know."

"Shut the fuck up Miranda, that's not what I mean," I snap, and Miranda rolls her eyes, "I've been seeing things."

"Oh great. Now you're a schizo. What are you seeing, dead people?"

"No. I've been seeing," I lower my voice as someone walks by, "I've been seeing bruises on people."

"What?"

"Like, I can see bruises and cuts on people. Some of them are blue and some of them are not and on me, they all are. Blue I mean."

Miranda stares at me, and I can see the skeptical look on her face. I can see that she's not keen on believing me.

"You've got a bruise shaped like a heart on your neck, or a hickey or something. And you've got a black eye."

"Which eye?"

"Left," I say, and Miranda's jaw falls open.

"Holy shit," her voice falls into a whisper and she tosses her cigarette on the ground, stomping on it.

"What?"

"The heart shaped hickey and the black eye? I had the hickey a few months ago when I was dating that guy James. He thought he was being cute. And the black eye? I've only had one ever, like 6 years ago. On my left side."

"What?"

Miranda stares at me, speechless. Then she throws her head back and laughs.

"Holy shit! You're fucking with me! Oh my god. You almost had me convinced. What else can you see Parker? How about the bruise on my shoulder you gave me when you punched me?" she laughs, pulling off her cardigan. I look at her shoulder and see it. The bruise is small, circular and blue. I look back at Miranda, frantic, but she's just laughing at me.

"Whatever the fuck you're on, I want some. You're a fucking psycho Ali," Miranda says, walking away from me. I watch her until she disappears into her car and drives away.

23

"Oh Sara? Sara are you in here?" I call out into the girl's bathrooms, being replied only by the echo of my own voice. I wait a moment, and hear a faint gasp and the sound of hands cupping over the mouth in an attempt to reclaim the sound. I smile and motion for Miranda to watch the bathroom door.

Amy moves towards the sink and sits on top of it, ready to chase after Sara should she try to escape. I begin to kick in the stalls, calling out Sara's name with every swinging door.

"You can't hide for long Sara, we know you're in here! Come out, come out wherever you are . . ."

I kick in the handicapped stall at the end of the bathroom. Sara is curled up on the toilet, hiding her legs in her sweater; face down into her arms that are folded above her knees. She look up at me, tears rolling down her cheeks, smearing the makeup that had once graced her eyelashes and eyelids.

"Please . . . Leave me alone, I don't want this," She whispers. Her voice is cracking. I smile at her and grab her shoulder, feeling her flinch under my touch.

"Oh come on now, I just want to talk to you!"

"Please just stop!" She is begging now, and I can hear the terror rising in her voice. Amy chuckles behind me, and I pull Sara out of the bathroom stall. She trips as she comes out and Amy grabs her, pulling Sara's arms around her back and holding her towards me.

I punch her, feeling her skin ripple underneath my knuckles. The impact causes my whole body to shake, and I smile at the feeling. It's an amazing sensation. I hit her again and again, each time feeling more and more alive.

"I thought you were my friend," she cries, flinching at the word, and the tears she had been trying to prevent from surfacing begin to pour out of her eyes. She sniffles, and starts to grind her teeth. She's shaking underneath me.

Amy lets go of Sara's arms, and she drops to the floor. I squat down to her and grab her face in my hands, forcing her to look into my eyes.

But her eyes are gone. They are black holes in her face with blue blood rolling down her cheeks like tears.

I toss her back, horrified. I try to scream, but no sound escapes my mouth. Sara stands up, her upper body limp. I look at Amy, who is covered in hundreds of glowing blue cuts. She is crying, dressed in all black and holding a single blue rose in her hands. The thorns pierce through her fingers, but she doesn't seem to notice. Sara steps towards me, her right arm extending towards me.

"You killed me," she whispers. Her voice sounds like a combination of herself as a little girl, herself as a teenager, and another, much more menacing voice. I stumble backwards, falling on to the floor.

"N-No! I didn't! You killed yourself you-"

I look at Sara again. She isn't the girl in high school that I kicked the shit out of anymore. Standing in front of me is a little girl with bright blue eyes and curly red hair that sticks out in every direction. She is wearing Sara's funeral dress, and etched into her arm, shining a bold blue and bleeding, is written the word; WORTHLESS.

"Ali, let's go out to play!" She laughs, and starts to move closer to me.

I back away from her, crawling on the cold stone floor of the bathroom.

"I don't want to play with you! Leave me alone!"

"Leave me alone. I don't want this," She says, mocking me in teenaged Sara's voice. She ignores me, moves closer.

I keep crawling away, and the cold stone floor sprouts thick grass. Headstones crawl out of the ground around me, and suddenly I back into Sara's headstone. I'm trapped. Little Sara stands over me, and places her tiny hand over my mouth. I can't control the noise that forces itself out of my lungs when she touches me, and my sobs thicken the air around me.

"Ali," she whispers. Tiny droplets of blue blood fall from her cuts and onto my legs. I look into her eyes. They are full of hatred, even with the innocence of a child. She smiles, and stares back at me, "It is your fault. You killed me."

I shake my head, whimpering under the coldness of her tiny fingers. I close my eyes.

When I open them again we are back in the bathroom, and I am staring into a pair of brown eyes filled with rage. Little Sara has transformed into me. I look down at myself to see the thick red sleeves of Sara's sweater.

I have become Sara, and I am staring into my own face. Into my own hateful eyes.

She looks at me, and acid on her tongue drips into my face and crawls into my ears.

"Why don't you do the world a favour Sara? Kill yourself you piece of shit."

I shoot up in bed, my forehead drenched in sweat. I look around my room. It is still and dark, and I am alone. I look at the clock on my bedside, squinting my eyes at the brightness of the glowing red numbers. 4:05 am. Great.

I want to lay back down, but I don't want to sleep. Every part of me thinks it's a bad idea.

It felt too real. The nightmare felt far too real.

I get up and go to my closet. In it I find a pink shoebox with frayed edges. I sit down on my bed again and run my hands over the cardboard. It feels surprisingly warm in my cold hands. I open it slowly. Inside I find pictures and mementos from my childhood. On top is a small doll, with curly ribbon as hair and a pink felt dress. Her eyes are blue buttons, and a pink smile is stitched across her face. I pick her up slowly and gently, as if she were made of porcelain. She looks worn down from the years, but as happy as she's always been. I find an immense amount of comfort in her smile.

"Hey little Sare-bear," I whisper to her, almost choking on the words as I say them. I can feel myself starting to tear up, but I force it back.

I place the shoebox on the ground beside my bed and curl into a ball around Sare-bear, my fingers entwined in her arms, until I fall asleep.

24

"Mr. Lewis will no longer be your teacher, he's left this job for personal reasons. I'll be teaching your class from this point forward," the new teacher Ms. Dean announces as she writes something on the white board. She's an older lady, somewhere in her late 40's and it's painfully obvious why she's not married. She looks like she's a raging bitch, and has a nagging voice that resonates in my ears long after she's done talking.

I slink back into my chair and look around the classroom. No one seems to be paying attention to her whiny voice either, instead being absorbed in whatever mundane thing they can find. I hear Nathan snicker behind me and I turn around to look at him. He notices me and smiles like a creep.

Fucking Nathan.

If I were any other girl I would be worried about him, but luckily I'm not. Nathan knows not to fuck with me.

Nathan raises his brow and his arm towards a girl sitting on the left side of the room. Her name is Charlotte Smits. She pretends to be popular, and we pretend she's our friend. It started in freshmen year when she approached us at lunch time. I smile a little at the memory. She was this nerdy little dark girl who no one particularly liked because she never shut up, but she was eager to impress us. Miranda was the one who got the idea of leading her on and pretending she was our friends. Soon we had lots of people believing it too, and a lot of girls playing along. She's practically our bitch, running around doing whatever we tell her to and acting mean to people. She's the only person we hated as much as Sarah, and even then we still liked her more.

Suddenly Nathan whips a wad of paper at the back of Charlotte's head and his friends chuckle. I look at them, and my attention draws to Gabe. He's staring at me, and I look away because I feel uncomfortable.

I look back at Charlotte and watch as she tucks strands of her pink hair behind her ears. I remember when we dyed it pink. We told her we wanted to give her a make-over for a party we were throwing, but we were really just screwing with her. We had originally intended to dye it green, but Amy's a fucking idiot and bought the wrong colour of dye. Still, it did its effect and Charlotte was horrified. She still comes around though, time and time again. She's the only person I've ever met who comes back to the people who hurt her with as much trust as the first time.

I watch as she reads the paper, her eyes filling up with tears that she tries to hide. I can't imagine what bullshit Nathan wrote, but I also can't imagine why he would write it to Charlotte. Charlotte was our joke, not his. He terrorized some nerd kid Luke and Sarah.

Sarah. That's why. Without Sarah there's no one lower than Charlotte to bully.

Then I notice something on her arm. Another blue cut, in uniform with other ones that are red. It sticks out, plain as day, to me. I stare at it, and wonder why it's blue.

That's when I get it.

Sara's cuts and her bruises were blue. Mine are blue. The bruise on Miranda's arm where I punched her is blue. The bruise caused by me. My bruises caused by my carelessness. Sara's body, blue to me and to no one else. Blue after she killed herself. Because of me.

It's blue because I caused it.

Sara and Charlotte cut themselves because of me.

I vomit when the thought comes to my mind. I can hear everyone in class gasp when I do. I caused it. It was me.

"Ms. Parker, are you alright?" Ms. Dean asks, rushing to my side. I can hear Nathan and his friends snickering. I vomit again.

25

When I get home I slam the door. My mother isn't on the couch, and I figure she must be out scoring or something. I can't hear Ben's sound system either, meaning he's out doing whatever the hell he does when he's not fighting orcs. In my head I thank Ms. Dean for suggesting I go home early, or I'd have to face them. I run up the stairs and into the bathroom.

I caused it. It keeps repeating in my mind, and I feel crazy because all I can hear are voices.

You caused it. You caused it.

You killed me

I almost vomit again when I hear Sara's voice replay in my head like it did in the dream, but I compose myself to stare in the mirror. I stare at the girl covered in blue marks and I feel disgusted and angry.

I start tearing off my clothes to stare at myself. The more layers come off, the sicker to my stomach I feel. Everything, every scratch and cut, is blue and I feel so alien. I open the cabinet behind the mirror and grab one of my shaving razors, then close the cabinet again and look into my eyes.

I cut my wrist, frustrated and unhappy. It starts to bleed a rich blue, glowing slightly.

Fuck. It's wrong. It's all wrong.

Blood is fucking red. Why isn't it red?

The alien hue of my blood disgusts and terrifies me and I start to cut more of my arm, growing more and more ferocious as I slice at my skin.

"Fuck! Just fucking be red! Fuck fuck fuck!" I cry, slashing my wrist with fury. My blood splashs against my face as slide the blade against my skin and as the air touches each open wound, pain shoots up my arm. I keep cutting, desperate to see droplets of red among the sea of blue blood that is dotting my wrist, rolling down my arm and splashing on to my floor.

"FUCK!" I scream, dropping my razor and taking hold of my wrist with my other hand. I collapse onto the floor, faint from losing blood. I touch my forehead to the floor and start crying, half from the intense pain and half from defeat.

I huddle into myself, crying and choking on my own saliva, feeling the warmth of my blood soak into my clothing. I have never thought of myself as someone who would self-harm, or feel the need to. I have always thought I was above it, that I was perfect; yet laying in my own blood as it pools on the bathroom floor I feel weak and terribly sad. I put my hand over my mouth, tasting blood as it seeps into my lips.

I feel so real, too. Angry and real and in so much pain.

"Ali?" I hear a voice ring from downstairs and I choke up. I don't immediately recognize the voice.

"Alison Parker?" I hear them call again, and I try to get up but I slip on my blood and I scream as my arm slams into the metal shower rod on the wall. The intruder runs up the steps and throws open the door.

"Ali!" he yells when he sees me. I try to cover my naked body but I can't move. I just cry and look at him. I feel as pathetic as I probably look.

He swoops down to me, grabbing one of the towels hanging on the door and covering me with it. I try to say something but all that comes out are gross choking noises.

"Are you okay? What happened to you?" he asks, his voice almost in a whisper. Then he notices the razor on the ground.

I look into his eyes and see panic. Then I black out.

26

I wake up warm and in a white room. I stare at the ceiling for a few moments trying to figure out where I am, until the flash of blue blood hits me again and I remember.

"Ali?"

I turn and see Gabe sitting beside me. I scrunch my eyebrows.

"Where am I?"

"You're at the hospital. After I saw you throw up in class I get worried and asked Miranda for your address. I found you in the bathroom . . ."

"Oh my god, you saw me naked," I say, looking back up at the ceiling a little embarrassed. Gabe stays silent, and I try to piece together what happened.

"You know, I understand that you were feeling guilty about what happened with Sara but trying to kill yourself won't solve anything. I was upset about her killing herself and I know I could have done something instead of acting like a pussy but I didn't. You shouldn't have been so cowardly and tried to," Gabe says, but I cut him off with my hand. It hurts to put it up, but I need to talk.

"I wasn't trying to kill myself."

"Then what the hell were you doing? You almost bled to death."

"I was trying something . . ." I say, trailing off in my own thoughts.

"Trying something? What the fuck could be worth risking your life like that?" Gabe demands. I look at him.

"Can you shut the door please?"

Gabe stares at me, his brow furrowed in confusion. Then he gets up and closes the door of the hospital room. He sits down beside me and gives me an expectant glare.

"You aren't the person I'd usually tell about this, but I tried to tell Miranda and it didn't work so whatever. The day Sara killed herself, I talked to her. In the bathroom. I didn't know it was her at first, but she knew it was me."

"What happened?"

"I'm getting there okay? She told me that I was the reason she was miserable, and I ran out of the bathroom stall to see her. But she looked different. She was . . . she was covered in blue cuts and bruises. At first I thought nothing of it and I just thought I was getting sick, but it hasn't gone away yet."

"What?"

"Not everyone's are blue. I think it's only the ones that are my fault. But there's a lot. I see them everywhere. And on myself . . ."

Gabe stops for a moment, thinking. I continue.

"I can see other ones too. They look normal, like they are brand new cuts and bruises. Like on you. You have a lot of bruises on your face. And your arms . . ." I stare at him. He shifts uncomfortably and covers his arms.

"The blue ones feel so unnatural and they terrify me. I just wanted to see myself bleed red again but I wouldn't. Every drop that came out was blue and I . . . I got out of hand I guess."

Gabe stays silent, and we sit together in silence. He slowly moves his hand towards mine and slips it underneath, taking it in his own.

"She was blue when I saw her at the funeral," I say, my voice hardly audible but I know Gabe heard it when I hear him inhale.

"What are you going to do?" he asks.

"I don't know what I can do," I say, "I'm scared I'll be like this forever."

"Nothing is permanent. Eventually, everything has to end. Some things just take longer to end than others, and some things end when we do."

"I should have ended everything I did to Sara before she did. Maybe then she'd be alive."

"Yeah. Maybe."

27

When I return to school, something is different. I can see the way people are staring at me in the halls, with malice in their eyes. It makes my stomach churn in the worst way, but I try to walk past without showing it.

"Can you believe she did it?" I hear a couple girl's whispering to each other and I freeze mid-walk. I turn to look at them, glaring. They hush immediately, and turn away from me.

"What did she do?" I ask loudly. They murmur and pretend they didn't hear me.

"I said, what did she do?" I ask again, and this time they close the locker they're standing by and walk away. I also walk away, feeling like I'm going to boil over.

I see Miranda and Amy in the hallway, talking to Charlotte and the other girls we usually associate with. When they see me they stop talking immediately, and I feel something creeping into my chest. I look at Charlotte's arm and see the blue again, and suddenly I'm painfully aware of the bandage on my arm covering my own cuts. I can feel them itching, but I try to push it back.

"Hey," I say, feeling a little apprehensive. Miranda looks at me with a disgusting look, and I clench my fist.

"What do you want?" she says, her voice laced with hate.

"Excuse me?"

"I said what do you want, freak?"

I'm as angry as I am hurt. Miranda has never spoken to me like this. No one has without me giving them a reason to regret it afterwards. I step forward, putting my chest out. Miranda scoffs at me. I've always been taller than her, but she's wider than I am and could beat the shit out of me. For whatever reason, she's never taken an opportunity to do that.

"Who are you calling freak, Miranda?" I say, trying to make my voice sound sturdier than I'm feeling.

"You, Ali. I'm calling you a freak. You're a fucking cutter freak just like the rest of those emo kids you used to think you were better then. Everyone heard about how you went fucking psycho on your arms. What are you trying to do, replace Sara after you killed her?"

Before I can rationalize I slam her against the wall, my knuckles pressing against her throat.

"You don't know anything Miranda! I didn't fucking kill Sara! It was never my idea to hurt her, it was you! You wanted me to hate her so you could have me all to yourself as a friend! You made me do it!"

Miranda pushes me off her, and I almost fall backwards.

"Me? Fuck off! Don't flatter yourself Ali. You're just as mean as the rest of us! You wanted to be popular and you thought she wasn't, so you told us to spread rumors about her! You wanted her to kill herself, remember? And now you're like her, you're fucked up in the head because you can't handle who you are. You're a bitch, and you have to live with it. You fucking killed her, get the fuck over it and get over yourself. You're a fucking psycho."

I open my mouth to say more, but Miranda is the kind of person who always wants the last word. She walks away, unapologetically, and I'm left standing in the hallway feeling defeated. Charlotte stays behind for a moment, and looks at me with panicked eyes. I look at her, and then at the blue cuts, and then back at her face. In one swift movement, she hands me an envelope and turns on her heel to run back to Miranda.

The front of the envelope has my name written on it, and when I open it I find 4 pages of paper. On the top of the first piece, written in sloppy handwriting, are the words: ALTERNATIVES TO SELF HARM.

I feel like I can't breathe.

28

The rest of the day goes by in a blur of whispers and snickers. By the end of the day I feel emotionally exhausted. By the time I can finally think, and really breathe, the only thing I want to do is cry.

I lay on my bed, looking up at the ceiling with the papers and Sar-Bear on my chest. I can't stop thinking about Charlotte. Why would she give me the time of day after the way I've treated her? In my mind it doesn't make any sense. I'm too sour for her kindness. I'm unworthy of anyone's kindness.

I look again at the sloppy writing on the papers. I can tell just by looking at the shape of the letters and the spots of rippled paper that Charlotte had written it when she was crying. I can't imagine why she would cry, but then again I can.

1. *Draw on photos of people and on magazines*
2. *Scream*
3. *Make tea and listen to calm music*

I stop reading. I can't picture anything but Charlotte trying to do these things to stop herself from cutting. She probably did these things after I hurt her. Sara might never have even thought about anything but cutting.

My hand crawls along the sheets of my bed until it finds my phone. I squeeze the cold device and bring it to my eyes. I suck in a slow breath, and start typing on the glass screen.

Me: Hey
Colten Shepard: What the hell do you want
Me: Can we talk?
Colten Shepard: Fuck no I don't want to talk to you
Me: Please. It's important.

Colten Shepard: It's not important enough to make me want to talk to a murderer

Me: Colten please

Colten Shepard: . . . . . .fine.

Me: Meet me at school, at the bleachers.

Colten Shepard: Whatever.

I get off my bed and try to will myself to look presentable. I put my hair up in a messy bun and throw a hoodie on, deciding against looking anything less than a slob. I can't be the Ali that Colten hates to look at right now. I have to be someone else, someone neutral to him.

I leave the house as fast as I can, avoiding my mom and brother. Nothing in me is ever ready to face my mother, especially when I have answers I need. As I walk towards the school I try to slow my breathing. My chest feels tight and constricted and I can't calm myself. Every step becomes torture.

And then I'm there, standing outside the fence that leads to the football field. I place my hand on the fence and look for Colten. He is sitting on the bleachers, staring at the field. Suddenly I feel terrified again, but still I move towards him. I stand in front of him, and force myself to speak.

"Hey," I say, breathless from the tightness in my chest. He looks at me, angry. I try not to let it bother me.

"Why did you want to talk to me?"

"I wanted to talk about her. About Sara."

"You don't deserve to talk about her."

"I know," I sigh and rock back and forth on my heels. He sighs, and I feel the awkwardness in the air. This was a bad idea.

We are there; together in silence, for what feels like a long time until finally Colten speaks again.

"Skin is a lot like the Earth. It starts off beautiful and untouched. It's a natural wonder. Then humans come along and destroy it, mark it up and change it. Cut roads into it. Every one of those cuts in her arm were a road to recovery, and every time a road got smoother you'd cut another one into her. You just kept cutting and cutting and now the Earth is destroyed and it can never be brought back to life. She can never be brought back. You destroyed her. You destroyed my world."

Colten puts his elbows on his knees and leans forward slightly, entwining his fingers and looking off into the distance. I sit down beside him, placing my hand on his shoulder. We sit in silence, watching the sunset. I have hundreds of questions but I can't find anything to say.

87

He turns to me after some time, his eyes watering but not allowing tears to come out. I take my sweater sleeve and wipe his tears away as they begin to escape his eyes. He looks at me, unsmiling and almost expressionless. The silence is too much, and questions scratch their way up my throat. They demand I ask them, and that they are given answers.

"I don't understand why. Why would she go to all this trouble? For attention? To get back at me?" I choke out, and I realize it's almost inaudible.

"No Ali, to feel something."

"Feel something?"

"The thing about it, you know depression? It's not just the feeling of being sad. Or hurt. It's a huge collection of feelings. And you get overwhelmed. And you're sad and angry and you don't know why, and you want to be happy but you can't. And you don't want to feel all these things so you hurt yourself to distract yourself from feeling. The pain of being physically hurt is a temporary relief from the pain inside your head. You don't know if you want to fix yourself or end yourself, and then you think that maybe self improvement isn't the answer. Maybe self destruction is."

I stare at Colten. His face hardens when we make eye contact, and he looks down to avoid me. I look at his skin. Little, insignificant cuts chipped into his face. He is like a statue; marble skin with cracks and chips from years of existence, but still beautiful to look at. The grass on the field moves with the wind, and it feels like it is the only thing that is moving in the stillness of the world. I look back at Colten. He looks so trapped without Sara, and his once radiating confidence has dwindled in her absence. He looks like a completely different person.

I realize that Sara isn't the only person I've killed. Metaphorically speaking.

"Colten . . ." I whisper. He moves his head slightly, only enough to look at me from the corner of his eyes.

"What?"

"I'm so sorry I took her away from you."

He chuckles, and I don't know what to say.

"You didn't take her away from me, she was never mine."

"I don't understand what you mean. You had feelings for her, didn't you?"

"Yes, but she was just a stupid teenage dream for me I guess. I know she never loved me the way I loved her, but I hoped. To me she was this beautiful mystical creature that transcended everything I could ever imagine, and I wanted her. I wanted her so bad that the minute she offered me her body I took it without a second thought and somewhere in my mind it made me believe I could make her love me back."

"And did it?"

"No, of course not. I was an idiot with her. I thought that if I could just make her love me her depression would go away. That if I was there, in her heart, she would magically be okay."

"People don't work like that, Colten."

"Well I know that now. I don't think I could have done anything to fix her depression, and even if there was something it's too late now. She's in a hole in the ground and she's never coming out of it."

I nod, still feeling a bit awkward. Colten leans back against the bleachers and looks up at the sky.

"How much did she hate me?" I whisper, hoping he doesn't hear me because I don't want to know the answer. Colten laughs a bit.

"She didn't, don't be stupid."

"What?"

"She didn't hate you. She hated who you became, but she always loved her Ali Parker. Even when I would talk shit about you, she was devoted to the You she loved. Every shitty thing Ali did was replaced with fond memories of her Ali-gater. It used to piss me off so much."

"I wish she would have hated me."

"So do I," Colten says.

"I wish I had never hurt her."

"So do I," Colten says again, his voice wobbly.

"I wish it was me in her place," I say.

He breaks down. His sobs fill the silence of the night, and his body wrenches in pain and sadness. It feels sick to watch him and not try to comfort him, but I can't will myself to touch him; to put my arm around him and hold him. Yet I feel something I had blocked out of myself for a long time stir inside me. Compassion, guilt. Responsibility for who I am and what I have done. I force myself to place my hand on his knee, rubbing it with my thumb in a feeble attempt to sooth him.

"So do I," he whispers between his broken sobs, and I start to cry too.

29

I watch as Colten drives away from the school, leaving me standing by the lonely flagpole in the front yard. When he leaves my sights I start walking back home, feeling a thousand pounds lighter than I ever have in my life. The sky is dark and the world is still, the trees unmoving black shadows along the sidewalk. Despite the chill of the air, I feel good.

Then, as soon as it came, my good vibes pass as I stop in front of her house. I bite the bottom of my lip and stare into the lightless windows. I can't see the cars of either of the Hale's in the driveway. Mrs. Hale left a few days after the funeral to live with her mother until they could find a new house. Mr. Hale, I have no idea where he could be, but the absence of his presence in the home gives me an idea.

I find myself walking towards the house and around to the side. It reminds me of the old days when I was a kid and I used to sneak into Sara's window whenever I was upset. I had done it hundreds of times, to the point where the lock broke and I could get in whenever I wanted to.

I stand under the window and swallow the lump forming in my throat. It's far up, so far that when I was a kid I used to climb in by the tree in Sara's backyard. But like her, the tree is gone, and instead I run at the house and jump in an attempt to grab the windowsill. When I finally get a hold of it I silently thank my genetics for making me tall, then hoist myself up. Carefully with one hand, I grab at the side of the window and try to force it to slide open. Then it moves, and I fall back onto the ground. I look up, frustrated at first until I see that the window has slid open just enough for me to pull myself through.

When I get in the window of her room I feel cold. Everything around me smells like her, almost as if she's never left.

It seems almost disgusting of me to mourn her the way I am. I mourn Sara like a friend would mourn a friend. I mourn a girl, who in many ways I killed, like someone who loved her.

I used to love her, I think to myself. She used to be someone I loved with everything I was. When I was the dirty kid with bruised elbows and a toothless grin she was the only thing that mattered to me.

I crawl up on her bed and curl into a ball. It still smells like she did when we were little. It reminds me of everything we did in this bed when we would have sleepovers. Her bed smells like the pink marker that she used to draw a port wine on my face so I'd look like her. It smells like popcorn and liquorice on movie nights and it smells like clean footy pajamas. My stomach turns, revolted at the smell. It reminds me that I betrayed my younger self by growing up to be me.

I wonder what my younger self would say to me now. No doubt she would scream at me and deny us ever being the same person. She would tell me I deserve to die just like Sara, and that I deserve to see everyone's scars. She would be as angry with me as I am, maybe even more.

I move my hand along the covers and try not to cry. I feel stupid and vulnerable like this, but I also feel like I need it. I need to be here.

My hand grips her nightstand, and it falls over. My heart stops, worried that the noise will wake up her parents. Then I remember that they are gone, and I calm down. I get up and pick up the nightstand and the drawer falls out, spraying its contents on the floor.

I start to pick them up until I find a journal with a sparkly unicorn on it. I bite my lip and hold it to my chest. I remember buying her this journal for her birthday. We both had one that we got for each other. We were supposed to write how we felt about each other in them, cataloguing our friendship until graduation where we would give them to each other as gifts. The one I have is in a box in my closet, and I make a mental note to myself to take it out when I get home.

I lay back on the bed and flip the journal open. On the inside cover is a picture of us when we were little, and I feel sick to my stomach. I turn the page to the first entry and start reading it.

Ali,

You are my bestest best friend in the whole wide world and I love you. You make me so sosososososo happy and I hope that we are best friends 4ever and ever!

Sara.

I turn the page again, and again, and again, and skim through hundreds of entries where she wrote about us and what we did together. Everything she wrote was positive, until the first day of middle school where all she wrote was "why".

I stop on that page and trace my fingers across the word. She was pressing hard on the page when she wrote, and I try to picture her when she wrote it. Then I push the thought out of my head and turn the page.

This is it. I can't do this anymore.

I stop reading and exhale deeply. I already know what this pencil smudged page is.

I thought for a long time that I could make it through high school. I thought that after my first and second attempts I wouldn't want to do this anymore but here I am. I never thought that I'd leave a note or anything; that's way too cliché of a dying person, but again—here I am.

I'm just too sad to keep going like this. Everyone at school hates me and it really feels like their mission in life is to torment me. I can't sleep without hearing their voices anymore, they are constantly talking to me and telling me I'm worthless. Even the voice that used to help me get through the day has turned on me and it's too much.

When I was 14 I wrote a poem about dead hearts. Dead hearts are the empty shells of people who lose themselves to something. It was stupid, but it was this explanation I had for myself about Ali. Ali is a dead heart just like I am, but she lost herself to popularity and image. I've lost myself to sadness. I've lost myself to myself, because at this point that's all I am. Sadness.

In the poem, I wrote that the dead hearts floated above the Earth waiting for the day they could return to the person they belong to. If they floated too far away, they could never come back and that person was lost forever.

That's what happened to my heart. It floated off so far that I can never get it back and now I'm here.

Mom and Dad, I love you guys so much. I know you both fuck up a lot and all you do is try to be perfect but you're not. I know I'm the reason you haven't divorced yet but now you can. You can both be happy without each other and find new people and you can heal. Without me, you'll have so much more to live for. I know that when you had me you were both miserable because you broke your purity vows and all that shit and got pregnant, and I know your marriage has never been happy. Take this as an opportunity to find the person you were meant to be with. You're both still young enough to start new lives and families.

Colten, I'm sorry you couldn't fix me. I know you cared but you went about it the wrong way and you need to fix yourself. You'll find someone, just don't try to find someone like me. Find a girl who loves you and isn't such a burden to you. Find someone who wants your friendship and who isn't always such a shitty downer.

Gabe, thank you.

And Ali . . . Ali I've always loved you more than anyone else. I'll always love you, even after what you did, but I can't forgive you. I'm a coward. I should have stood up to you and told you how I felt about how you were acting but I couldn't. I'm sorry I wasn't cool enough to be your friend, and I'm sorry that I made you hate me so much. I wish it could have been different but it can't.

This is it, and I'm not scared. I died a long time ago.

I pull the journal close to my chest and let myself cry. My chest feels hollow.

I curl into a ball and stare into the room. And as I lay in the stillness of an unending darkness I think about the dead hearts floating over the Earth, and I wonder how far away from me mine has floated.

30

I wake up to the chirping of birds and the sound of people shouting downstairs. I fly out of bed, freaking out because I'm not at home and the Hales shouldn't be either.

"Kathrine, you don't understand what I'm going through right now!"

"What you're going through? What you're going through, Ted? She wasn't just your daughter, she was my daughter too!"

I crawl slowly towards the door and push it open with my fingertips. I can hear Sara's parents loud and clear in the living room.

"You haven't been here for me since I found her! You ran off to your mother's and left me to mourn for my daughter alone! I've needed you and you abandoned me!"

"Get over yourself Ted! Do you think I could stay in this house? Do you think I could stay here with you when you haven't given me a fond look in years?" Mrs. Hale's voice is broken and whiny and I think that she might be crying. I hear Mr. Hale laugh.

"You never deserved a fond look! You slept with another man, you broke our sacred vows!"

"Oh don't you bullshit me about your sacred vows! You got me pregnant in high school! The only reason we ever had those vows is because you felt bad about having sex! If you would have stuck with your sacred vows we would never have been in this mess!"

"Sara was never a mess!"

"She was, Ted! Our marriage is a mess and she was a mess! You tried so hard to pretend she wasn't! We both knew the person she was, don't pretend you don't. You didn't want to admit you had a sad daughter, and you definitely didn't want to admit your daughter liked girls."

"Don't talk about her like that!"

"Stop denying it! You've always known she had romantic feelings for Alison Parker when they were little and you pretended she didn't! You knew she liked girls and boys and anyone she found attractive and both of us denied that. And when she was depressed we told her to get over it because you wanted to be perfect, but guess what Ted? You're not. And I'm not. And I'm leaving you so you can find a way to be perfect. Without me and without our daughter."

I hear Mr. Hale sigh and sit down on one of the squeaky couches in the living room.

"We were happy once," he says, his voice wobbly.

"You were happy once. Sara was happy once. With you, I've never been happy."

Then I hear the door close and the low sobs of a broken man, and my throat closes up. As fast as my legs will carry me, I run for the window. Then I stop, because I see Ali-gater; the doll Sara made of me and Sar-bear's counterpart. Without thinking I grab her, then go to the window and lower myself out.

I collapse on to the ground underneath the window, clutching Ali-gater to my chest. I close my eyes and move my fingers through the soft yarn hair and wonder for a moment if Sara ever did the same. It feels like something heavy is on my chest, weighing me down.

I hear a gentle meow, and open my eyes. Sara's fat cat Lou is sitting on my chest, staring at me.

"Hey Lou," I coo at him and he purrs, rubbing his head against me. I hear tires screech, and look towards the road to see Mr. Hale speeding off in his car.

"Looks like you're locked out, huh? Did you come out here to get away from the fighting?"

Lou jumps off me and starts walking towards the edge of the yard. When I don't follow him, he turns to look at me and meows.

"You can come stay at my house. My mom will be too out of it to notice."

31

Lou lays at the foot of my bed, purring like a maniac, with his paws pressed against the soles of my feet. I watch him intently, trying to block out my emotions, and twist my cellphone in my hand. Lou perks his ears up and sighs.

"Me too, buddy," I say, leaning my head back. I check the screen of my phone again. I texted Gabe almost 10 minutes ago, hoping he would call me. No such luck.

Then the phone rings, and I excitedly pick it up.

"Hello?"

"Hey, you wanted me to call you?" Gabe sounds confused. I would be, too.

"Yeah. I just wanted to talk to you I guess. About Colten and stuff."

"Colten? What about him?"

"I, I uh talked to him yesterday," I say. Lou gets up and walks to my hand. I scratch the top of his head.

"Oh? Did he punch you in the face again?"

"No, not this time. We talked about Sara mostly. About me."

"And how did that go?"

"It went okay. I don't think he'll ever forgive me but at least he talked with me," I sigh.

"Is that what you want? Forgiveness?"

I bite my bottom lip. In many ways I think I do want forgiveness. Forgiveness for being as awful as I am would have been great, but Colten can't be the one to forgive me.

"I don't know," is all I can respond with. I hear Gabe sigh.

"What do you want then, Ali?"

"I want to be normal again. I want things to go back to the way they were. I don't want to think of myself as such a monster and I definitely don't want to be one."

"Well, things can't go back to how they were because Sara is dead. There is no way to change that now. But you can be normal again, you don't have to be a monster."

I laugh, because it almost seems preposterous.

"And how do I stop being a monster? How do I become normal, Gabe?"

"You're the one with that power. Talk to the people you've hurt. Make yourself better."

"I can't do that."

"Why not?"

Because I'm scared to, I want to say. Instead I hang up and toss my phone on the floor.

Make myself better? He says it like it's the obvious solution and the easiest thing to do in the world. How can I even manage to be anything but a piece of shit? I've been like this too long to change. Changing would mean becoming something I'm not. I'm not a good person, and I can't make myself one. I don't want to sacrifice who I am.

That's how I became this way. I sacrificed myself to become popular. I sacrificed my friendship with Sara to be with Miranda and Amy and all the other girls who I thought would make my life better. And it did until now. Everything was perfect for me until Sara killed herself.

It makes me hate her. It makes me hate her so much for ruining my life. It makes me hate myself even more for ruining hers.

Lou meows at me, sounding small. I look at him, and he stares back at me.

"I wish you could talk, Lou. I need someone to talk to about this."

For a moment I think Lou nods, but I realize that I'm just going crazy. He crawls over me and goes to my bedside table. He picks up Charlotte's papers in his mouth, then puts them on my chest. I am going crazy.

"Talk to Charlotte? No way Lou."

Lou stares at me. I'm arguing with a cat.

"There's no way that talking to Charlotte about anything will make this better. I bullied her more than I bullied Sara. She probably hates me."

Lou puts his paw on the papers. I'm actually arguing with my dead neighbour's cat.

I sigh in defeat and frustration. Lou starts purring. I argued with a cat and lost. Maybe Miranda is right. I am a fucking psycho.

"Tomorrow," I say at Lou, who responds with louder purring. I turn over into the fetal position. Lou crawls over me and wiggles himself into my arms. I fall asleep with his chin pressed against my cheek and his hot breath on my skin.

32

I wake up with cat drool smeared down my face, but despite that I feel good. Then I hear my mother screaming, and I feel like a ten ton weight has dropped on me. It seems like waking up to disasters is going to be my new thing.

Lou hisses, and I fly out of my bed and down the stairs. I see my mother in a puddle of herself on the living room floor, tears and snot running down her face. I can see the pinpricks of needles and scabs all over her arms, and I want to vomit. But instead my mouth goes dry and I get down on my knees to get eye level with her.

"Mom?" I say, unsure if my words are even getting through her thick skull. She looks at me with glassy eyes.

"Ben's left," she says, her voice cracked like she hasn't spoken in years.

"What?"

"Ben's left," she says again, completely indifferent.

"Why?"

"That fucking ingrate said that I was a bad mom. He told me he hated me," her voice is sour and laced with anger.

"Where did he go?" I ask. I feel like an idiot, asking simple questions, but I just can't process Ben leaving. I can't process Ben leaving me with my train wreck of a mother.

"Fuck if I care," she slurs, and I try not to burst into tears. Why would Ben leave without me? He knows how much I hate living with her. How scared I am with her around. She tries to get up and stumbles, placing her bony hand on my shoulder. I revolt backwards, vocalizing my disgust with her touching me.

"What the fuck is wrong with you?" she growls at me.

"Don't touch me."

"Help me up you little shit," she tries to put her hand on me again.

"Don't touch me!"

"What the fuck? Help me up."

"No, I don't want to."

"Don't act like this to me. You're lucky I even let you live here. You and your ungrateful brother."

"Mom, you're not supposed to treat us like this!" I scream. She looks like she's going to hit me, and I flinch until I realize she won't. She's too high to hit me. For the first time in my life I silently thank her drug dealer.

"You don't get to tell me how to treat you, I'm your mother!"

"Then act like it! You've been nothing but a drugged up loser since dad left," I stand up. Towering over her I feel like I always did in school; I feel powerful. Looking at someone from above makes me feel powerful, but this is the first time I feel like this power is clean. My mother scoffs.

"I don't deserve this treatment you give me, mom. I don't deserve to be ignored by you. I've done a lot of shit in my life, but I don't deserve this."

"What are you going to do about it Alison? Where are you going to go?"

It takes everything in me not to hurt her. That's how I deal with it; I hurt people. I beat them down until they can't hurt me anymore. But I don't want to hit my mother and cause disgusting blue bruises on her body. I don't want to live knowing I hurt another person.

So instead I run back upstairs and into my room. I can hear my mother screaming at the top of her lungs downstairs, but I block it out as I stuff clothes into a back pack and pick up Lou. I go to my closet and grab a tin of money that I've been saving up since I was younger and stuff it in my bag. My mother used to steal any money she found, so I made my money tin with Sara to hide anything I made from her.

When I've taken all I can carry I go back downstairs with Lou in one arm and my keys in the other.

"Where the hell are you going?" my mother snaps at me. I clench my hand around my keys.

"I'm leaving too."

"Whatever, Alison. You've got nowhere to go."

I clench my teeth and try to keep myself from screaming at her. I look at her face for the last time, and see myself. I look like her, every feature a match for hers. But I am not like my mother. I won't end up alone like this. I won't allow myself to end up alone and angry like she has.

I leave the house without speaking another word to her, and get into my car. I put Lou in the passenger side and drive away from the place I called home for the last time.

I understand now why I have to make myself better.

"Want to go talk to Charlotte?"

Lou meows, and I smile. I smile because I won't allow myself to cry over my mother anymore. I smile because I can be better.

33

I've been waiting outside of the school for over an hour with Lou in my car, petting his head as he sleeps. I check my phone and sigh. I had asked Charlotte to meet me here and, despite her obvious confusion, she had agreed to come. I stare out the window, feeling impatient and afraid. Afraid because I will have to apologize, and afraid because after this I will have nowhere to go.

I see a flash of pink hair coming down the street and I swallow hard. Charlotte looks as rough as Sara did on the last day I saw her. Her hair is in a messy up-do, and she's wearing a baggy sweater and sweatpants. I roll down my window and wave to her. She notices me and waves back, quickening her pace. In my mind I ask her to slow down, but she quickly is at the door of my car. She opens the passenger side door and sits down.

"I didn't know you had a cat," she says as Lou promptly takes a seat on her lap. She puts her hand on his back and he purrs.

"Yeah. He adopted me yesterday I guess."

"Cats will do that," Charlotte says, laughing. She feels awkward, I can just tell. I clear my throat and start my car.

"Coffee?"

"Yeah, that would be great."

I look at Charlotte and see the subtle glow of blue under the arms of her thin sweater. On her neck I can see bruises climbing up to her jawline, ending on her cheeks. Apart from the light bruises there, her face is relatively clear of marks and cuts. I look at her for a little too long, and she turns to look at me. I turn away, feeling embarrassed, and start driving.

"So, can I ask you why you wanted to talk to me? I mean, I know that we hang out a bit but I've always had the impression that you didn't really like me," Charlotte asks, her voice getting progressively quieter as she talks.

"The papers. And your arms."

"What about my arms," she chokes out, then clears her throat.

"I saw your cuts. That's why you gave me that list, isn't it?"

Charlotte stays quiet. I take in a deep breath.

"I know that they—or at least one of them—was because of me. I know that I hurt you. We all did with our bull shitting and pretending to be your friend, and I'm sorry."

Charlotte looks away from me, obviously trying to hide her face in case she starts crying. I wish I could do the same.

"We should never have used you the way we did. You are a person, not some stupid toy for us to fool around with."

"What brought this on?"

"What do you mean?"

Charlotte looks at me, still looking confused. She gestures towards me.

"What brought this out of you? You've never been the type of person to apologize for being an asshole. You've always been so . . ."

"Selfish?"

"Rude. Sure that your treatment of others was justified. Powerful, really. Why so different now? What changed in you?"

"Hurting myself. Sara. I don't know. I just . . . I know I need to be better."

"Oh."

"I can't make excuses and say that I never meant any of the shit I did, because I did mean it. But I can honestly say that I'm sorry that I did it, and I'm sorry that you felt so much hatred for yourself because of how I treated you," I say, my voice failing as I talk. I can feel sobs slowly rising up my throat and I swallow to keep them down.

"I know how it feels to be angry and afraid now and I had no idea that it could take so much out of a person. That the need to hurt myself could be so urgent in the heat of the moment."

"Yeah. That's how I felt for a long time."

"I'm sorry I made you feel that way."

"It wasn't just you," Charlotte laughs, then falls silent for a moment again. She wants to make me feel better but I don't. I still feel awful.

"Depression can do that to a person. It's just this unending void of emotions that sucks you in when you least expect it. One day you think you've gotten out and away from it, and the world seems like it's decent for a little while, and the next day it sucks you back into the darkness. It's just easier to get sucked in when everyone around you pushes you in, or at least it feels like they are," she says, looking up while she talks. I've never noticed the curves of her lips before, and how they move into a heart shape while she speaks.

Looking at her, I can't even imagine why we ever considered hurting her. Miranda used to say it was because she wasn't as pretty as us and that she was weird. In a lot of ways she's not as pretty as I am or as Miranda, but she's still pretty in her own ways.

Charlotte turns to look at me and catches me staring again. This time I don't stop.

"Have you ever considered ending it, like Sara did?" I whisper. I want so desperately to know if I could have ended another life without even realizing. Charlotte nods.

"I was going to do it today, but then you called me."

"What?"

"I had planned to do it today. I guess... I dunno I just guess that Sara did it kind of made me feel like I could. I mean, she's had it so much worse than I have but I knew that Nathan was relentless with her. The note kind of scared me, and there's just been a lot of shit going on at home. I feel like I'm losing grip on myself and reality and- god I'm sorry I'm boring you with all this."

"No, I want to hear. I mean, I don't seem like the best listener but I want to me. I want to know."

"Oh, okay. I guess really it's just been so many things piling up on me that just makes everything seem so bleak. For a little while I thought that I was going to be okay, but then the depression got worse and now it just feels like I'm never going to be normal ever again. I keep telling myself that if I get out of my house and into my own place I'll be happier, but then I think about how much more likely I am to kill myself if I'm alone."

"Why do you hate being at home? Is it your family?"

"No! Well, kind of. I mean, they're really great people but my brother is a tyrant. He does everything he can to screw with me and my parents just let him. And they get so mad when anything about my depression comes up. They figure they have enough on their plates already because of my siblings, and that I shouldn't be so much work since I'm the oldest. It just stresses me out."

I nod in understanding, and the awkward silence comes back. I look at Charlotte, and she looks down.

"Do you really think that if you're alone, you'll off yourself?"

Charlotte shrugs her shoulders and looks at me with tears in her eyes. I pull over and park the car, unbuckling my seatbelt. Then I hold her as if she were slipping away from life right then, and she cries into my chest. I hold her as if letting go would allow her to slip into the void, as if my arms were the only thing holding her down to this world. She keeps sobbing, clutching the fabric of my shirt with her shaking hands. I cry too, because I can feel her pain. I can see her pain, and it's changed me. All it took was a bruise to show me who I was, and I as I hold Charlotte in my arms I decide that I can live with those bruises. If it means knowing that I can be better, I can live with seeing bruises every day of my life.

"I won't leave you alone, okay?" I say into her hair.

"I don't know if you can promise that, but it's a nice sentiment," Charlotte whispers.

34

"Gabe?" I say into the receiver of the phone, hoping that Gabe hasn't fallen asleep on me. He replies with a tired grumble.

"I left my house for good. Do you think I could come crash on your couch? I don't know where my brother is."

"Why did you leave? What's going on Ali?"

"It's a long story. Can you ask your parents?" I beg. Gabe coughs on the other end.

"I live alone. You can come. I'll text you my address, ok?"

When I get to Gabe's apartment I linger outside. Lou meows at me, expectant. I want to hiss at him, but instead I get out of my jeep and send a text to Gabe telling him that I've arrived.

He comes out of the front door with messy hair and pajama bottoms on, scratching his head. I smile at him, and he waves at me.

"I hope you don't mind, but I brought someone," I say as I open the passenger side for Lou. He jumps out and starts rolling around on the cement sidewalk. Gabe's face lights up.

"Smelly cat! Hey buddy!" he says, squatting down to pet Lou's belly, "Where did you find this little guy?"

"Sara's house. Her dad abandoned him so he's adopted me."

"He knows a good person when he sees one," Gabe says, and I cough awkwardly. Gabe stands up and opens the doors to my back seat, grabbing my bag for me. I pick up Lou and follow Gabe to the door.

His apartment is what you would expect an apartment owned by a teen boy to look like. The furniture is mediocre and old, with only a couch and a lawn chair gracing the living room. His TV is quite large and expensive, and he has videogames set up on an old coffee table in front of it. His window is covered by bed sheets with ridiculous cartoon characters on it, and if it weren't for it being open I feel like it would smell odd in the house. The kitchen is small and littered with dirty dishes and minimal cooking ware, but the place feels more like home than my house ever did. It feels and looks like someone lives here, and it makes my heart race.

Lou jumps out of my arms and makes his way over to the tacky flower patterned sofa. I take off my shoes and walk in, staring further at the house.

"Sorry, it's a little messy," Gabe says, obviously embarrassed.

"No, it's fine. It's very nice."

"Thanks. The bathroom and bedrooms are down the hall. There's a second bedroom but there isn't a bed or anything."

"How can you afford this place?"

"I got my mom's estate after she died, and after that I took on a lot of part time jobs. I wanted a place for my sister to come home to."

"And will she come home? Will she come here?"

Gabe laughs and shakes his head. I decide to drop the conversation when I see tears forming in his eyes.

"I'll only stay for a while if that's okay with you. A few days tops, just until I can find my own place," I say, trying to assure Gabe that I won't infringe on him for long. Realistically, I don't have an idea where I could go. I have no friends and no job. My only friend is a cat, whose owner I killed. I'm only completely pathetic.

"You can stay as long as you need to. Who knows, you might make the place a little brighter. Do you want something to drink at all?"

"Yeah, what do you have?"

"Tap water or beer."

"I think I'll go with the beer."

"Ohhh underage drinking. Naughty, naughty," Gabe laughs, going to his fridge. I take a seat next to Lou and lean back.

"You can smoke in here if you want to," Gabe says, and I silently thank him in my head. I just need something to ease my stress for a moment. I feel like the world is moving too fast and I need to catch up.

Gabe comes back with two cans in his hand and tosses me one. I open it and take my cigarette out of my mouth to take a swig. It tastes like wheat and ashes, and I love the combination.

"So, why did you leave your house?" Gabe says, taking a drink from his can. I sigh.

"My mom is a crack whore and a psycho, and my brother left without me. The first time he leaves his room in ages and he forgets to take me with him. My dad did the same thing to me when he couldn't handle my mom's addiction. One morning I woke up and he was gone, and today I woke up and Ben was gone."

"My dad left me too, when my mom was dying."

"My mom's not dying," I snap.

"She will be," Gabe says quietly.

I want to say something snarky back, but I know that he's right.

"Don't worry Parker, I'm not going to force you into sad back story mode just yet. I'm going to get you drunk first so you're more tolerable, then make you spill all your secrets to me."

"I'm sure that will work well for you," I laugh, taking a long puff from my smoke.

"Oh you better believe it will Parker."

35

"Would life really be that different if cows had wings?" Gabe looks at me, but I can't focus on him. He's just a haze of colour.

"That's one of the stupidest questions I've ever heard in my life," I say, feeling my words trip over my tongue. Lou jumps on the coffee table, knocking over empty beer cans and liquor bottles. I don't remember how much I've drank.

"Just hear me out okay? Like, if birds and cows switched places would life be different?"

"Okay, switched places how? Are cows staying the same size or becoming the size of birds?"

"Bird-sized."

"That would be so cute. I would keep one as a pet."

"You're really weird Parker."

"I'm weird? You're the one talking about bird-sized cows."

"I'm drunk!"

"I'm drunker than you are and I'm completely not weird," I laugh, smacking my knee with my hand. I feel good. Hazy and slow, but good. I look at Gabe, who is staring at me with glossy eyes. He looks like he's going to kiss me, or he's just drunk. For a moment his face looks normal and bruise free, but then they reappear and I almost cringe. Even when I'm drunk I see scars.

"You know when you're like this I understand why she loved you so much."

"What do you mean?"

"Sara. When we talked, she spoke so nicely about you, and how great of a friend you were. I never understood why until now."

"Oh. Thanks I guess?"

"Yeah. Ali, you're not as bad of a person as I thought you are. Well, you were. You were a total bitch and a half."

"Oh. Thanks I guess."

"But now you're really changing. It's nice, it's good. I like this version of you."

"I think I do too but I don't know. I don't feel like me when I'm not hurting others. I've done it too long, it's engraved into my soul like some kind of ancient tablet thing. I'm a bitch at heart."

Gabe leans back on the couch.

"We are all mean at heart. Humans are the meanest creatures in the world. We shit on anyone we think is below us and cause wars over skin colour and money and who we fuck."

"Amen."

"But we are also creatures that are capable of compassion and empathy. In a lot of ways we are just stupid little animals waddling in drunken stupors under a sky we can't even imagine. We all know we will eventually die so we eat, drink and fall in love so we can feel some kind of meaning in ourselves."

"Philosophical. Where are you going with this? Or are you just drunk?"

"I'm drunk, but there is a point here. You're no longer that shitty person you were, or at least you don't need to be. But in the grand scheme of things, I think you had to be that person to discover who you are. Sara meant something in your life, didn't she?"

I try to push away the cloudy booze from my mind to think about her. I see her face in my mind. Her as a child, her as a teenager. I picture her here with us, and as an adult. Then it becomes to much, and I try not to think about it.

"She should have been the person I grew up with. All those experiences I had with Miranda should have belonged to Sara. My first drink, my first boyfriend, the first time I went camping without my parents. The parties and the heartbreaks. I should have experienced those with Sara. She should have lived the way I've lived."

"You could also have had your first lesbian sexual escapade with her," Gabe chimes in, giggling. I almost drop the drink cup in my hand.

"Who told you anything about that?"

"Sara might have said you almost or did kiss once. She wouldn't tell me which was true. Maybe you should?"

"Oh my god," I bury my head in my hands, flustered. Gabe laughs, probably guessing the answer from my reaction.

"Now that's sexy."

"No, oh my god it wasn't like that. There wasn't a kiss I swear to god. Even if there was, there would be no 'lesbian escapade'."

"Oh? Why not? Not into girls?"

"No! Yes? Shut up! It's not like that, it's just that Sara didn't like sexual stuff."

"How would you know? You weren't friends with her in her teen prime."

I laugh at Gabe and he looks at me confused.

"Okay, first of all; girls don't steer clear of their bodies until a boy comes along in their teen years. We were twelve and talking clit, alright? We were discovering ourselves, and Sara discovered that she didn't feel the need to do it," I say, still laughing a bit. I take a sip of my drink and the strength of the alcohol burns my nostrils. I have no idea how much booze is in this.

"But she had sex?"

"Yeah probably. But I can't say I haven't had sex to escape how I was feeling."

Gabe contemplates it for a moment, then nods.

"Was it because she was molested by your neighbour?"

"No, that wasn't the reason. I think she was always like that. The incident was just a sick infringement on a young girl."

"What happened to the guy?"

"He moved I think. Never got persecuted for it. If I knew where he was I'd probably kill him though."

"I hope you find him one day," Gabe laughs, and I laugh with him.

"Me too."

For a little while we are quiet, drinking more and more. My mind is clouded with booze and smoke, and when I look at Gabe again to speak I feel as if all of time has stopped.

"I talked to Charlotte,' I say. I feel like my words are coming out one per minute. Gabe raises his eyebrows in surprise.

"How did that go?"

"It went good. I felt better after. I apologized to her, almost cried. She's really pretty have you ever noticed that?"

"So you do like girls!"

"Girls can say other girls are hot."

"Boys can't."

"Boys are stupid and need to affirm themselves."

Gabe laughs louder than I thought possible, and it spooks me a little. I put down my drink.

"I do like girls. I think I like girls more than I like boys, but I like boys too."

"Awesome. I like girls too."

"No joke huh?" I laugh. I yawn, and realize how tired I actually am. Gabe yawns too and stands up. In a fluid motion he takes my hand and gets me to stand up from the couch with him, leading me to his room.

I lay down with him beside me, with the world dizzy and broken. I look into the darkness of his room and for a moment I swear I can see my dead heart floating back to me, and it lulls me to sleep.

36

I wake up still drunk, but it feels good. My mouth on the other hand, does not. It tastes horrid, like someone vomited booze and butts into it. I feel Gabe move in the bed and hear him moan.

"You know, this is the first time I've ever woken up on a Monday with a strange girl in my bed."

I turn to look at him, and when we are face to face our noses almost touch. He smiles a goofy smile and sits up. I sit up too and look at the clock on the wall. It's 10:30, so we're late for school, but with the weekend I've had I don't even care anymore. Gabe gets up and starts putting his jeans on. I didn't realize he had taken them off while we were in the bed together.

"Well, hurry up Parker. If we are lucky we can still make our last morning class."

"Do I really have to go? I've had a really bad weekend and," I fake cough, "I'm sick."

Gabe laughs and pulls the blanket off me. Reluctantly I get up and walk out to the living room to get my bag. Lou is sleeping on it, and starts purring when I attempt to move his fat ass.

"Come on Lou, get up," I say, hoping I don't look like a complete psycho for talking to the cat. Finally he gets up and jumps off, allowing me to take my bag to the bathroom.

When I open my bag I realize just how little clothes I brought with me, and I immediately wish I had brought more. I put on a pair of jeans and a t shirt and stare at myself in the mirror. My bruises are dimming, and for the first time in what feels like a long time I look like Ali Parker. Not just the teen Ali Parker, who I've grown to know and hate, but the teen Ali Parker who I've grown to forget. I smile and start brushing my matted hair, then decide to shower and wash it.

After about 10 minutes, Gabe calls me. I shake my hair in a towel and get dressed again. I open the bathroom door and walk out to meet Gabe.

"You look ravishing."

"I look ravished. Let's go, I've missed a lot of school lately and I really just need something normal right now."

"Fair enough,' Gabe says, opening the front door.

When we arrive at school I hurry to class, making it in time. I can't seem to focus my attention on the lesson though, and I find myself going into a robotic sort of mode until lunch. When the bell rings and I go to the cafeteria, I immediately feel like an outcast. I can see people staring at me, especially Miranda and the other people I used to call my friends.

Amy leans over to Miranda and whispers something, and they both laugh without taking their eyes off me. I don't look away from them. I stare them down, unwavering and angry. Then I hear the crashing of plates, and I lose my focus.

Nathan and his friends laugh as a short fat kid named Jake falls on the floor. I can see from where I'm sitting that his food tray has scattered across the floor, including where his body has hit the ground. He stands up, his clothes smudged with ketchup and potatoes, and tries to walk away. Nathan has other plans, and instead grabs the back of his shirt collar.

I can hear the snickers and hushes around the cafeteria, and I feel like I'm watching a lamb get pulled into the jowls of a wolf. The other sheep don't want to intervene for fear of being eaten up too. It reminds me of the times I was bullying Sara in plain daylight. People watched and whispered, but no one helped her. They laughed with me, because they were afraid of me. The girls I became friends with only did so because they were afraid and wanted the power I had. Nathan only respected me because he knew I could hurt him more than he could ever hurt me. Now Nathan is the alpha of the school because I lost my nerve, and that's why I'm sitting alone and watching him show others he's taken over.

So I stand up.

"Hey Nathan," I say. Nathan takes a moment to stop bagging on Jake to look at me. Still ugly as ever, he smiles the disgusting grin I've grown used to seeing whenever he hits on a pretty girl.

"Well look here! Parker decided to return from the psycho house. Heard you slept with my buddy Gabe last night you slut."

I look at Gabe, who's sitting at the table where Nathan is. He gives me a sorrowful look, but I know it's bullshit. Gabe is like the sheep too, afraid to cross the people who can hurt him.

"Stop being an asshole. Let Jake go and keep to yourself," I say, trying to sound stern. Nathan lets out the grossest laugh I've ever heard.

"Do you even hear yourself?"

"Yes, I do. I'm trying to eat lunch in peace and you're being an asshole. Why don't you just stop?"

"Stop?" Nathan keeps laughing. I want to run over there and hit him. I want to push his squished up nose straight into his skull. Instead I just stay standing, staring him down.

"Stop being mean to people, what the fuck is wrong with you?"

"I've got to stop being mean to people? Did you hear that guys! From the queen bee herself! Ali Parker thinks I'm too mean to people," Nathan and his friends laugh. I look back at Jake, who is staring with me in disbelief. Under the thick rims of his glasses I can see the glowing red of an old shiner on his face, and tiny ticks of red on his lips. Worst of all I can see his arms, lined with multiple horizontal cuts. Among them is a long jagged line, glowing a bright electric blue. My bottom lip starts to tremble, and I look into Jake's eyes again before turning to Nathan once more.

"Yeah, I do Nathan. Leave Jake alone, what has he ever done to you?"

"What did Sara Hale ever do to you? How about Charlotte? Everyone knows you only pretend to like her! No one thinks for a second that you're sincere about your sympathy, no one. Who's really the mean one here Parker, you fucking two year old."

"I stopped being like that. I'm not like that anymore."

"What did that? Sara killing herself? What do you feel bad about anyways? She deserved it."

"How dare you say that? You—you take that back."

"Fuck no. You said it yourself 100 times! She didn't deserve to live."

I push Nathan with all my strength. I'm furious at him, and holding back angry tears as I stare into his eyes with hatred and fury.

"SHE DESERVES TO LIVE MORE THAN BOTH YOU AND I! THEY ALL DESERVE TO LIVE A HELL OF A LOT MORE THAN WE DO—JAKE, CHARLOTTE, EVERYONE ELSE WE'VE HURT-THEY ARE THE ONES WHO DESERVE SO MUCH MORE THAN US!" I scream. I can see the reactions of everyone when I stop talking. They all think I'm a psycho. Miranda snickers.

"Whoa there queen bitch calm the fuck down!"

"No! I won't calm down until you fucking leave Jake alone, he doesn't deserve this shit!"

Nathan gets up, pushing Jake out of his way.

"Fuck this shit. I don't have to answer to you Ali. Let's ditch guys, we can resume our quality time with Jake later," he says, and the others at his table get up and follow him. Gabe doesn't move.

"No," he says, glancing at me for a moment.

"What the fuck dude? Did that skank's pussy make you a fucking fag? Let's go."

"Ali's right dude. You've got to stop this bullshit. We won't have quality time with Jake later, you're just going to beat him up again and—I'm not going to be a part of it."

"Whatever dude, you used to be cool," Nathan says, starting to walk away.

"No, I used to be a coward. Cool isn't sitting around and watching you pick on people. I'm sick of it! Every class you write some shitty note to someone and harass them. I don't want to be a part of that. That's the kind of shit that got Sara killed."

I can hear people gasp in the cafeteria. I look around at them. I know they blame me for her death, no one will say it though. No one wants to admit they did anything wrong. In the crowd I see Charlotte staring at me.

"Alison being a bitch killed Sara," Miranda scoffs. I look at her and sigh. I feel so defeated by her. Charlotte shakes her head at me, and I smile at her. At least someone doesn't think I'm awful.

"I know you all blame me for it, and I blame myself too," I say. I feel weird, talking in front of so many people. But looking at Charlotte and Gabe, I feel strong.

"I know in a lot of ways I've killed parts of you guys too. I'm a bitch. I'm an awful person with no sense of right or wrong and I look down on all of you. And I've known that for a long time. But I've learned too. Since Sara killed herself I've learned things. I know how many people I've hurt. I can see now."

I look out into the cafeteria and see the scars. There is blue everywhere, but this time I don't feel guilty or afraid. I feel ready.

"I'm sorry that I couldn't see until now just how many of you I've been hurting. I'm sorry that I couldn't see that a lot of you were hurting already. I know now that we all bear scars of our lives. We have scars of our emotions branded on our bodies, and we bear them. A lot of you walk around with smiles on your faces even with these scars, and I know it may not mean much coming from my but I am so proud. I'm so proud that you're still here, and I'm sorry. I'm sorry that I've put a lot of you, including Sara, in the position where you felt hated and scared. Hopeless . . ."

"You don't have to forgive me. Hell, I don't expect you to. Sara won't. Sara can't. But I do hope that you can find it somewhere in yourselves to forgive me. And to change too. No one ever stopped me. You all watched each other crumble under me, and that's just as bad. I know no one wants to take the blame, but we all killed Sara together. I killed her with violence, and you killed her with silence. We all could have saved her, but now we can save each other."

"This is fucking cute and all, but no one cares," Miranda says. Amy and a couple other girls laugh with her, and I sink into myself. That's when Charlotte stands up, her arms coated in blue.

"I do," she says, her voice clear and unafraid.

"I do," Gabe repeats.

"I do," I repeat too.

"Me too," says another voice. I turn around and see Colten standing in the doorway of the cafeteria. I feel my knees trembling, but his solid face reassures me. People whisper about us, about the boy who could be called the dead girl's only friend. He looks at me and nods, and I smile at him.

Then, slowly but unwavering, the rest of the students in the cafeteria stand up and a course of "I do's" rings out. I watch in shock as they rise, standing together with pure determination on their faces. I feel like I'm going to faint, but Charlotte comes towards me and grabs my hand. I hold it, steadying myself on her support. Colten walks over and grabs my other hand, and soon we all join hands. I look at Miranda and Nathan, who stare at the mass assembly of people in front of them. Joe, Cam and Amy all join us too, abandoning Miranda and Nathan.

Then I break down into tears and fall into Charlotte's arms. She comforts me as I did her, and I feel forgiven by the people I've hurt.

All but one.

37

6 Months Later

We pull up at my house. It's quiet and it looks like it's abandoned, but beyond the dust forming on the porch, it's the same old house I've always known. I look at Gabe, nervous to go in, but he smiles at me and gets out of the truck. I get out too, following him to the front door of what I used to call my home.

The door is unlocked, and when I go inside I already know that no one is home. Inside it smells like rotted food and dirt, and I scrunch my nose up as I climb up the stairs.

"Where's your mom?" Gabe asks me. I shrug.

"God knows. She probably went out to score or something." I say.

"No, she died," Ben says, coming out of his room. Without thinking I run to hug him, but I stop short.

"Dead?" I ask. Ben nods.

"She overdosed. Died in your room. I got here a couple of days ago. Came to get my stuff and you, but she was already gone by the time I got here."

I don't know what to say to Ben, but with the look on his face I know we are both feeling the same way. Relieved. As much as I loved my mother, she's always been toxic to us and herself. It's sick, but it's the only thing I can feel for her. I mourned the loss of my mother a long time ago.

"I couldn't get a hold of you at all. I wanted to tell you about it. And I wanted to let you know that I'm selling the house. I don't want it, and I don't want the memories this shit hole has."

"Good. I'm sorry you haven't been able to call me. I disconnected my phone after I left. Couldn't afford it anymore. Where are you living?"

"I have a place up in the city. Gotta job up there too."

"Oh cool."

"Ali I'm so sorry I didn't come back for you sooner. I should never have left you with her."

"It's okay Ben, I know," I say, hugging him.

"Do you have a place?"

"Yeah, she's living with me. We have a cat," Gabe says. Ben smiles awkwardly and I laugh.

"We're just stopping by to grab the last bit of my stuff. There's something I forgot here that's really important and I've got to return it to a friend," I say. Ben nods and ushers towards my room. I leave Gabe and Ben in the hallway and go in.

It's odd being there again after being gone so long. Odder that this was where my mother chose to die. But I'm determined, and I search the room for what I need until I find it. I pick up the delicate shoebox and blow dust off the top. My heart is racing as I open it, revealing the two little cloth dolls inside, scattered among photos and journals. I pick them up and move them to my rucksack, then close the lid of the box and carry it out.

"What's that?" Gabe asks. Ben sees it and smiles, ruffling my hair with his hand.

"Let's go. I don't want to be late. I'll see you again Ben?"

"Yeah Ali-gater. I'll give you my number so you can call me. You'll need to keep in touch if you want a penny from this shitty old house."

We laugh together and hug. He walks us to the door, scribbling his phone number on a gum wrapper as we walk. When we reach the door he hugs me again, lingering.

"I love you kid," he whispers to me. I kiss his cheek.

"I love you too, dork."

When Gabe and I get in his truck I sigh.

"Are you ready to go?" he asks me. I nod.

"As ready as I'll ever be."

38

"Are you sure you want to do this? You don't have to if it's too hard."

"I need to though. I want to."

Gabe smiles weakly at me and opens the door on his side of the truck. I open my door too, and feel the chilly wind surround me. It's a cool autumn day and the wind is slow. As I step on to the gravel road of the cemetery it picks up for a moment and blows my hair into my face. Gabe walks around the back of the truck to stand beside me. I look at his hands, which hold the flowers I had picked earlier in the morning to bring here with me. I reach back into the front seat of Gabe's truck and grab my old rucksack, and sling it over my shoulder. I look back at Gabe and half smile, and we start walking. The cold win tingles against my fingers and I retreat them into my bright red sweater, sticking my hands into my armpits.

We walk through the cemetery, passing gloomy graves ordained with withering flowers, melted candles and washed out pictures. Stray leaves on the path crunch under our feet, providing breaks in the eerie silence of the cemetery. Everything around us is death; dead leaves, dead silence, dead people, dead hearts. I don't like being here.

"It's over here," Gabe finally says. His voice is heavy and breaks as he talks. I stop on the path and watch him approach a tiny headstone that lay in the middle of a row of much larger ones. Compared to those around it, it seems rather bright; new. It's void of flowers or candles and has no photos or memorials, but it's clear to me who lays there. The headstone has a carving of an angel on it, her wings breaking off the sides as if she were ready to take flight. Her eyes are blindfolded, but I can still see the painful expression her face is contorted into beneath the blindfold. She holds her arms out, holding a banner in her hands that I assume reads the name of the deceased, but I don't bother to read it. The pale blue glow of the headstone tells me that Sara is buried here.

As the gloomy sky greys more and more, and the pale blue of Sara's headstone harmonizes with it. To my eyes it is highlighted, reminding me of my mistakes. I look at Gabe and watch him as he places flowers on her grave. They provide a splash of colour to the dreary world we stand in.

We stand in silence for a long time, neither Gabe nor I daring to speak. I bite my lip and stare at the angel. I think to myself how glad I am that she's blindfolded. She can't see the sinner that stands before her. I'm not very religious, but I'm afraid of her judgement. Afraid that she would be angry that I'm here, standing above Sara like I had done so many times before. I try to reassure myself that it's different now. I'm not here to hurt her; I've already done that far more than I could have imagined I would.

"Are you ready to go?" Gabe says, clearing his throat. I look into his eyes and shake my head. I can see that he's holding back tears.

"I think I'm going to stay here for a little longer. I want to talk to her. Alone. I'll uh, I'll see you back at the truck?"

"Yeah. I'll be waiting."

I wait until his footsteps are merely an echo before I move from my spot. Soon he's gone and I relax my stance. I sit beside Sara's headstone and take my rucksack from my shoulder, placing it on the ground at my feet. I rifle through it until I find them; two apple juice boxes and two cloth dolls. I squeeze the little red headed doll in my palm and set her on my lap. The blonde doll I place on Sara's headstone, along with one of the juice boxes. I breathe deeply, pulling my knees up to my chest and hugging them as I lean my head against the headstone.

"Hey Sara. It's Ali. I'm not sure if you can hear me, but I just wanted to . . . I was cleaning out my old room and I found our dolls. Do you remember them? We made them in like, grade 3 and you didn't like yours because you thought it wasn't pretty enough to look like me, and I was upset that the red yarn wouldn't curl enough to look like your hair," I laugh and start to open the straw wrapper on my juice. My hands are trembling as I fumble with the plastic,

"Those were the days, huh? We used to drink apple juice on the playground before bedtime and the future. We were going to be best friends for the rest of our lives together . . . I guess I ruined that though, didn't I?

"Sara . . . I'm so sorry. I'm so sorry for everything I did to you. I'm a jealous idiot and I lost sight of who we were. You were my best friend—the best thing that ever happened to me, and I abandoned you. I was so selfish, and I thought I was above you. That Miranda and Amy were somehow better than you. They are never there for me like you were, but somewhere in my thick skull I thought it would be a good idea to abandon you. I'm an

119

idiot. A terrible excuse for a person and I—I'm trying really hard to change that. It's hard though Sara. Sometimes I pretend I haven't done anything but I did so much of that before too. When I first saw what I did to you I tried to ignore it. I pretended I couldn't see it, or other people hurting you. And then you . . .

"If I had stopped them, stopped myself; would you still be here? If I had just apologized when I saw your cuts instead of pretending I hadn't, would you forgive me? I know you would, you've always been so forgiving. You didn't even hate me. Gabe told me you didn't. He told me that you still loved me until the end. I don't know how you did that, but thank you. I love you too Sara. I'm sorry that I forgot that."

I start to wipe away the tears that drench my face with the sleeve of my sweater. I grab the juice box from the headstone and open it, then set it back down in its place. I take a long sip from my juice box and let out a sigh, trying to calm myself down. It's gotten dark, and I squint to see better. The only light in the cemetery is a lonely streetlight. It flickers on and off, and moths circle around it in a frenzy. I laugh and run my hand through my hair.

"You were scared of moths when we were-"

I stop mid sentence, and stare at my forearm. My skin is pale and covered in freckles, but the glowing blue cuts and bruises that I had from cat scratches and rough housing are gone. I drop my juice box and frantically search the rest of my body, lifting up my clothes and looking into the reflection of my phone to see my face. The only marks on my body are my freckles, age spots and the occasional pale scar. My power is gone. I start to cry again, with astonishment and joy rather than sadness. I clutch the tiny cloth doll I had made of Sara in my hand and hold it close to my chest, crying longer and harder than I ever have in my life.

"Ali!"

I look up to see Gabe holding a flashlight. It's dark outside, and his face is stricken with worry but bare of cuts and bruises. I jump up from the ground and into his arms, sobbing loudly.

"Ali, are you okay? I was getting worried and—why are you crying?"

"It's gone—I can't . . . I'm"

"Hey, hey, calm down. You're fine. Everything is fine."

"Yeah," I sigh out between sobs. Gabe and I start to walk away from the cemetery. I hold the cloth doll close to my heart and move closer to Gabe. He keeps one of his arms around me as we walk. Though the night is silent and the wind has stopped, as I look back to Sara's grave I hear a whisper in her voice, as if she were sitting there, saying;

"I forgive you."